The Patterns of Paper Monsters

"*The Patterns of Paper Monsters* is a dispatch from the teenage wasteland of a juvenile detention center, fervidly delivered by Emma Rathbone's irreverent, perceptive, and achingly funny young hero, Jacob Higgins. He refuses to succumb to the numbness and absurdity of his incarceration, in turn holding a jagged mirror shard to adolescence, failed relationships, and life in modern America. A voice that is at once heartbreaking and hilarious, and startlingly true."

— Lydia Peelle, author of *Reasons for and Advantages of Breathing*

"No matter how loudly I praised *The Patterns of Paper Monsters*, no matter how many classic coming-of-age stories I compared it to, the unforgettably sarcastic and broken and endearing narrator, Jacob Higgins, would no doubt roll his eyes and show his teeth in a smile that was more of a snarl and say, 'Can't you do better than that?' And I would want — as I wanted so many times when reading this debut novel — to slap him upside the head and strangle him into a hug. And you will feel the same way, utterly charmed and disgusted, ultimately moved, when you read what promises to be one of the best books of the year by one of our best new writers, Emma Rathbone."

— Benjamin Percy, author of *The Wilding, Refresh, Refresh,* and *The Language of Elk*

THE PATTERNS OF PAPER MONSTERS

a novel

EMMA RATHBONE

A REAGAN ARTHUR BOOK

BACK BAY BOOKS

Little, Brown and Company

NEW YORK   BOSTON   LONDON

Reagan Arthur Books/Little, Brown and Company
Hachette Book Group
237 Park Avenue, New York, NY 10017
www.hachettebookgroup.com

First Edition: August 2010

Reagan Arthur Books is an imprint of Little, Brown and Company,
a division of Hachette Book Group, Inc. The Reagan Arthur Books
name and logo are trademarks of Hachette Book Group, Inc.

Library of Congress Cataloging-in-Publication Data
Rathbone, Emma.
    The Patterns of paper monsters / Emma Rathbone.— 1st ed.
        p. cm.
    ISBN 978-0-316-07750-7
    1. Teenage boys—Fiction.   2. Juvenile delinquents—Fiction.
3. Juvenile detention homes—Fiction.   4. Adolescence—
Fiction.   I. Title.
    PS3618.A84P37 2010
    813'.6—dc22   2009047398

10 9 8 7 6 5 4 3 2 1

RRD-IN

Printed in the United States of America

To Alena

THE
PATTERNS
OF
PAPER
MONSTERS

The Media Center, or "Choices"

I'm sitting in a cold room next to a girl named Denise Henly who is making wet sounds with her mouth. Every time I manage to drift off into some daydream tributary, she snags me with the slippery jostling of her tongue or the smacking of her lips. I can't really figure out what she's doing and I don't want to turn my head to look, possibly causing her eyes to lap up against mine. And besides, I'm just trying to sit here.

It sounds like her head got turned inside out. But when I think about it, I figure the only explanation could be that she is engaging in some sort of habitual grooming regimen. So finally I risk it and pretend to look at the clock but really look at her and she's like, very efficiently biting her fingernails, which are painted a chipped silver like she's an obsolete technology from the future; some kind of discontinued android assassin. So now I'm picturing us at the end of the world. She's gyrating on top of me — wires twitching and spewing out of her severed synthetic arm as hostile searchlights invade our holdfast.

I can't help but notice I'm freezing. I'm sitting beneath an overbearing spiky plant at computer number four in the euphemistically titled Media Center. You would think that a room called Media Center would have a lot of high-tech crap in it: some flat-screen TVs, some scanners; some crouching, stream-lined staplers. Well, it doesn't. It does, however, have nine com-puters at various levels of sophistication—except they are all so slow they might as well be made out of tile—set up on a few flimsy seminar tables, hovering over a snake pit of cords and a number of angry adapters.

I also can't help but notice the poster on the wall next to the door has been changed. The old one depicted a little puppy stag-gering around in some spilled paint and invited the viewer to "Get Inspired." The new one is of a man wearing a bright yel-low visor, standing on a mountain precipice and surveying the expanse of land beneath him. On the bottom, in a big classy-looking font, it says, "Choices."

I close my eyes. I feel hungry and cold and sick all at the same time. Some machine, somewhere, jolts on, and an electric hum falls on everything like a blanket of snow. A yawn courses through me. I hear a voice. I try to ignore it but it persists, worm-ing its way into my aural field and whatever section of my brain triggers disemboweling irritation. It is the voice of a woman. A woman who for some strange reason, some fucked-up glitch of circumstance, happens to be able to tell me what to do. It is the voice of Mrs. Dandridge.

Mrs. Dandridge

Mrs. Dandridge is a pile of a person who smells like someone's weird house. She wears clothes with many layers. She makes a big deal out of getting up and sitting down. She is, due to some vague history in law enforcement, in charge of the computer room. She is also in the business of making me want to punch things. The way she says my name, all smug and unwinding, as if she has me summed up and pinned down like a display beetle, makes me want to punch the sky. And then punch the sun for crowding the sky. And then punch a door and maybe a step-mom. She is always reading paperbacks with apocalyptic titles like *Last Days* and *Skygate*. Her bookmark is a little laminated prayer with a purple tassel on it.

"Jacob *Higgins*."

I turn around.

"Yeah?"

"Would you please approach the desk?"

I push my chair out and approach the desk.

Something else I've noticed about Mrs. Dandridge is she always wears earrings that are different things. For instance, one earring will be a little dangling tennis ball and the other will be a racket. Or one will be a paintbrush and the other a little palette. I would like to go ahead and carpet bomb whatever tiny real estate in my brain contains that information.

I get to her desk and she looks up like she's surprised to see me and sort of annoyed she has to put down her book, which has a bunch of people on the cover looking skyward at a crown of thorns made out of clouds.

"What's *He Went Down On Me* about?"

She goes, "The book is called *He Came Down*."

"On me."

"And . . . *excuse me?*"

I don't say anything and she conspicuously looks over at Officer O'Connell, who's idling in a chair in the corner.

She goes, "Am I going to have to call Officer O'Connell?"

"No."

I might as well mention one of the main features of life here at the JDC, of what it's like just standing in a room or next to a desk, which is the quietness, or rather the presence of this administrative, test-taking, ambient ebbing and flowing tide of coughs and minor shifts in paper. It's like a sickening anti-silence that's worse than actual silence, and it's the opposite of nature and it makes everything you say, every conversation you have, sound stale and reheated.

"May I ask why we didn't sign an honor slip today?"

Mrs. Dandridge sometimes falls into that side road of condescension where she refers to things in the collective.

"We didn't have a pen."

She nudges forward a tin with about twenty uncapped ballpoint pens in it.

"These pens are here, every day, right next to the honor slips."

"Oh, yeah."

An *honor slip* is a bookmark-size slip of colored paper, depending on what day of the week it is, that you're supposed to sign when you come into the Media Center, that says, "On my honor, I pledge that I will use my computer privileges responsibly and refrain from seeking out material that is inappropriate or not related to academic research." As if you have a choice about what to look at (which you don't). As if you aren't already prevented from looking at anything slightly suspect by the software they've installed, indicated by the pixely padlock graphic that flashes on the screen when you log on (which takes about a year, and if you type too fast, the computer has five seizures and has to reboot). As if by just touching a computer you are stepping into some dystopic black market with busted neon signs flickering in the rain and cyborg hookers trying to solicit you at every corner (I wish) and you are walking stoically through it all because you're so honorable with your signed honor slip. So the whole thing is this dumb charade of free will, which, I don't really care. It's just that I get sick of signing them every day with a gravelly ballpoint

6

pen so that Mrs. Dandridge can stick them in that red binder and eventually file them under "Who Gives a Shit?" in some cabinet in the sky.

Mrs. Dandridge takes a slip out of the little plastic bin and pins it down to the desk in front of me. "Please be so kind as to sign an honor slip right now."

"Can I ask you a technical question?"

She lifts up her book and puts her bookmark in it and lays it back down in a series of motions that can only be described as agitated.

"What is it?"

"If I don't sign this piece of paper, will my honor still be intact?"

She shifts in her seat. "Excuse me?"

"Because I don't know how I could face my people if my honor wasn't intact. I don't know how I'll be able to procure the sacred wind clover that would ultimately save my people."

We both look over at Officer O'Connell, who is now looking at us. Dandridge recomposes herself and fixes her eyes on me. She nudges the slip forward on the desk.

"Sign it."

"You're not going to answer my question?"

She leans forward. "Mr. Higgins. You are wrong if you think this conversation is going to last much longer. You will either sign this honor slip or I will call Officer O'Connell."

Something brushes against the computer room door and we both look in that direction. My eyes fall on the new poster, of the man standing on the mountain. "Choices." Half the land below him is covered in a shadow. He is staring out with a nondenominational look of contemplation.

I get a pen and lean over and sign my name really small, which causes Dandridge to furrow her hideous brow.

"That's too small."

"It's my signature."

"It's unreadable."

"You can't read it?"

"No."

"I can read it."

Now she's got her eyes set on me with a look I'm sure was meant to be leveling, and maybe would have been if I was like, twelve years old and not 170 unhinged, haphazardly raised, possibly bipolar juvenile pounds with only the most tenuous impulse of civility (cultivated in spite of an upbringing that taught me otherwise many times) keeping me from punching her in the stupid, doughy face.

At this point it's really quiet. People are watching. She takes the slip, tears it up, and lets the pieces seesaw down through the air and into the trash. She gets another slip from the little plastic bin and shoves it in front of me.

"You will sign this slip with your regular signature."

I just stand there.

I'm dribbling this experience across the dumb stadium of the universe and I will slam-dunk it into a yawning black hole and then everyone will die.

I'm a tall glass of water, filled to the very top, trying not to spill myself.

She says laughingly, for show, "Are you with us, Mr. Higgins?"

And that's what does it. The way she says my name. That's what causes me to overflow. I'm still holding the pen. It's like all that boring, antiseptic time in the computer room was cranking my arm back. And now it releases, springs forward, with the local violence of a rubber band snapping. The pen comes down hard on something soft, almost doughy. Someone screams. Lights out.

Lights Out

My name is Jacob Higgins. I'm seventeen years old. It was about three months ago that I woke up from a fibrousy Klonopin haze to find myself standing on the steps of this building, at the beginning of a punishment that, I'm sure you would agree, far outweighs the crime.

I stood there looking at the Barbecue Tavern on the corner of the street. The sky was gray. Officer O'Connell was shifting his weight from one leg to the other. A plastic bag rolled by like a tumbleweed. I was trying harder than I've ever tried to do anything to force myself back into my haze, but I couldn't because it was like a blanket that was getting smaller and smaller and eventually went away and then I was more wide awake and confused than a spider in the middle of a flickering television screen.

Finally the door clicked open and thus began the Olympic trials of boredom and grudging acquiescence that now define my life. I saw a woman I would eventually come to know as Jan, who had a clipboard and who was talking to me, and I can't remember if she was asking me questions or just *telling* me things.

My eyes were stuck on a staple embedded in the blue carpet. When I looked up I saw a man with a bunch of folding chairs walk by. The woman in the receptionist booth or whatever it is leaned over and said to Jan, "Gerald is going to be late again." Then Jan looked at me and straightened out her face and handed me over to Aaron, as in, "I'm going to go ahead and *hand you over* to Aaron, who will show you how this place works," but not before giving me a booklet entitled *Rules and Procedures* and saying, "It's your responsibility to read this."

And that was my first helping of the microwaved rhetoric this place dishes out on a numbingly regular basis: "It is your *responsibility*" (people like to say it all slow and mouthy as if you're deaf) "to be ready for bed by lights-out." "Your group will suffer the *consequences* if the trash cans in the rec room aren't emptied out." "What part of the *decision-making process* compelled you to rip all of the pages out of my desk calendar?"

Portrait of the JDC

I was then led through a concert of doors—smudgy revolving doors, glass doors, heavy wooden doors with frosted windows in them—and deposited in my "room," where I lay down on my bed and stared at the ceiling and started breathing really fast before I realized that there was really no point in doing that. But rather than describe the psychotic carousal of anger and deadened acceptance I experienced that night, here is a portrait of the Braddock County Juvenile Detention Center.

Heralded by a massive parking lot, the JDC is the center of a series of gray buildings, interspersed with crappy, East Coast, monotone pine trees, that make up the judicial area or "court system." This area also happens to be next to downtown, which they are trying to reinvent as some sort of Dickensian old town square, complete with colonial-style parking booths and the aforementioned Barbecue Tavern.

I had driven past this area a million times and never knew, or ever really wondered, what it was, because why would anybody care about a concrete pile of Tetris-shaped buildings in the armpit of northern Virginia in the early twenty-first century? Here is the answer: they would be *forced* to care about it when they found themselves being tamped down into it so that Braddock County could take a giant bong hit off them and be really proud of itself for "rehabilitating" people.

I'll say this for the JDC: it is well lit. There is light everywhere. Beams of fluorescent light flood the painted cinder-block hallways at all times, casting a surgical brightness so that you can see the green in people's eyeballs, which is gross.

I'll also say this for the JDC: it exceedingly accomplishes the task, like most buildings, of being a series of rooms.

We spend a lot of time in the rec room. It's laid with torn, dusty carpeting and is haphazardly occupied by a number of things: a Ping-Pong table, a few caved-in sofas, a television and DVD player. There's a disparate selection of posters on the wall that have nothing to do with anything—including one depicting a man, possibly homeless, wearing a suit of strung-together soda cans. On the bottom in a casual handwriting-style font it says, "Be Yourself." There's the always-empty snack bar. And the bookshelf containing such classics as *WordPerfect for Beginners* and a *Far Side* desk calendar from 1998. My favorite aspect of the rec room happens to be the dusty, yellow, octagonal chairs at each of the tables, obviously left over from some half-assed design initiative who knows how long ago. And let's not forget the mounted whiteboard (in case the impulse strikes you to give an off-the-cuff presentation), which is inexplicably surrounded by burlap curtains. The walls of the rec room are painted a palliative green.

You've got your cafeteria, a pale landscape of folding tables and chairs. You've got your computer room, which I've already mentioned. Then there are our rooms where we sleep. Simple. Sparse. A bed slab. A metal sink and toilet. A trash can, a mirror, no window except for the one that looks out onto the central common room. A very low ceiling that seems to be made out of some sort of flimsy corkboard that has little specks that writhe like tadpoles if you stare at them for too long. My room is made up of a spectrum of unpleasant whites—sterile-wall white, stained-pillowcase white, boring-September white, I-wonder-if-I-could-hang-myself-with-this-sheet white. It's a white fist of . concrete. The anteroom to a crumpled piece of paper.

Most things happen here on the half hour. The lights click on at seven-thirty in the morning. Then it's breakfast until eight-thirty. Class goes until two-thirty with a half hour lunch break thrown in at eleven-thirty. Vocational training or electives go until four-thirty and on and on and on, with the day whittling down to me here, writing in this stupid notebook until half the lights click off, whereupon I lie with my eyes open and try to slam my brain shut in the dimness that is meant to approximate nighttime.

Or if you happen to be in lockdown, which is where I was for the past forty-eight hours, you get to exist, solitary confinement–style, in your room with nothing going on except for a counselor peevishly looking into the little window in your door on the half hour to make sure that you aren't killing yourself.

Lights out.

Lights out.

Lights out.

I Hate It Here

I hate the sticky scraping sound everyone's issued sneakers make on the linoleum floor. I hate the pebbly white-painted cinder-block walls. I hate basically every aspect of the way everything looks.

I hate the smoke detector in the rec room, which no one seems to be able to fix and which emits a shrill little beep every five minutes. And that on the whiteboard is a half-wiped-out draw-ing of a piece of pie that was probably part of some lesson in

1972, and no one will ever erase it. I hate the food here because it feels hostile.

I hate having to see Lane every week. I hate how Pastor Todd always tries to high-five me in the hallway. I hate how even though lights-out is supposed to be at nine-thirty, the lights always go out a little bit before then. I hate being hungry all the time. I hate being sleepy all the time. I hate how when the lights click on in the morning and I wake up, I always kind of feel like I'm not really here, and then it always turns out that I am really here. And it always feels the same—like I fell down some sleep chute and have been *deposited* into the morning.

I hate sitting in classroom 107A and listening to Roy Hassle give his half-drunken soliloquies on the Civil War or whatever. I hate our soft-papered, floppy homework workbooks. I hate the girl on the cover of our soft-papered, floppy homework work-books with her huge sweater and the passport she's holding up and the fact that she looks really fertile and grateful and some-times I'm attracted to her.

I hate that I always have to pee. And I always have to pee the most when there are about five hundred reasons why I won't be able to pee for another hour—I'll be in the computer room or the rec room, and Aaron or Jake or whoever will be too busy to escort me to the bathroom, or I'll be in class, where you're basi-cally not allowed to pee because you should have taken advan-tage of your "bathroom privileges" when you had the chance. Which brings me to another thing that I hate, which is that someone is always watching you. You get maybe two or three times a month where circumstances conspire to give you even a moment of privacy, and then you roll it up and smoke it real fast and get stoned into thinking that you're a normal person on a normal day, until someone is like, "Why are you...shouldn't you be in the cafeteria?"

I hate how Aaron always speaks in rhetorical questions: "Did I *tell* you to put that notebook away before lights-out?" "Did I *ask* you whether you wanted to sweep the main room carpet or not?" I hate our list of revolving chores—emptying out the trash cans in the rec room, sweeping the floors, washing the bathroom mirrors, straightening out the shelves.

I hate the fact that life sucks so hard here that the revocation of certain "privileges" actually constitutes punishment. Like if you mouth off in the cafeteria, you have to miss movie night (I can't believe I don't get to see the exciting conclusion to *Mrs. Doubtfire*). Or if your room isn't sufficiently clean in the morning, you don't get to go to snack time (which legitimately blows).

But the thing I hate the most, more than anything, is the cold. It is always cold in this building. The air that comes out of the vents is like glacial wind swept up from prehistoric ice dunes. In the computer room, the rec room, here in my own room, the cafeteria, the hallways; it's not a minty, sterile kind of cold. It's an ancient, haunting cold that is always just short of freezing my balls off. My hands are cold, my hair is cold, the dirt underneath my fingernails is cold, the slime on my eyeballs is cold. I'm cold when I'm writing, I'm cold when I'm adjusting the sheet on my bed slab, I'm cold when I'm eating, I'm cold when I'm just fuck-ing *standing* there and I think it's giving me brain damage and I fucking hate it here more than anything.

I am now going to try and imagine myself enveloped by pil-lowy fields of warm labia.

Portrait of Lane, My Therapist

I'm sitting on a denim couch, looking at a large candle with twigs embedded in it.

"What are you looking at, Jacob?"

"That candle."

Lane twists around and stares at it. "It was a gift from my sister."

"It has twigs in it."

"Yes."

I shift in my seat. A gust from the air vents causes some dream catchers to flutter against the bulletin board.

"Well... *why?*"

Lane recrosses her hands. "It's decorative. My sister makes them. She puts twigs in them and sometimes leaves and sometimes" — she looks around — "cranberries."

"Oh," I say. "It's a good thing someone's doing that."

Lane begins to say something, but I go, "What if they catch on fire?" I put my hands in my armpits to keep them warm. "What if it melts down to that part and the twigs catch on fire?"

Lane readjusts the folder on her lap. "It's not really meant to be lit," she says.

"Good." I look around. "Because I really wouldn't want this place to burn down."

Coasting in here on a tide of sand-colored stationery every Friday is Lane Davidson, who, by virtue of a degree from Magazine University and a number of billowy linen outfits, calls herself a therapist.

I am supposed to see her once a week. Every Friday, Officer O'Connell escorts me to her office next to the cafeteria, where I find her sorting through some folders or playing another thankless game of Solitaire on her computer. When she finally senses something, she looks up and then back and forth between me and Officer O'Connell, as if she's mildly surprised, as if we *haven't* been coming here at the same time for the past however many weeks. Then she looks at her watch, then looks up at me and says, "Fine. Hello, Jacob."

Let me just put it this way: everything in her office is made out of denim or is denim-themed. The couch I sit on has a denim pillow with an actual pocket on it, like a jeans pocket, like it thinks it's Bruce Springsteen or something. There is a picture on her desk of what I'm assuming is her fat little kid with a denim frame around it.

My thoughts are not provoked to a higher level of self-analysis by the dream catchers hanging from the bulletin board. Or her collection of pleasant calendars. Or the purple vase with tons of little cracks on it that you can tell are intentional, holding dried willow burs (or something, I don't know what they are, but they're some crackly western-looking flower).

Neither are my thoughts provoked by her constant tapping of her pen on her clipboard and the expression on her face which can only be identified as the harried boredom of the dissatisfied middle-aged woman in an administrative position who is just waiting for an opportunity to wield some of her baby boomer straight talk.

Our conversations (when I even decide to say anything) are a series of the same crappy ballads accompanied by Lane clicking her pen and me sighing. Sometimes we improvise with some dueling silences to keep things interesting. Our biggest hit is "You Should Be on Antidepressants."

"Jacob," she'll say, "have you ever considered that your mood swings might have something to do with the chemical makeup of your brain?"

Silence.

"Jake, you seem to have been in some sort of low-grade depression ever since you've been here."

Silence.

"Do you think that's true?"

"Yes."

"Why?"

"Because I'm in a fucking juvenile detention center."

"Please do not swear at me."

Silence.

Sometimes her cell phone will ring. And when it does, the same thing always happens. She gets flustered, starts rooting through her huge bag (made out of denim), takes it out and holds it at arm's length like it's trying to attack her. She jabs some buttons until it stops. Her hair is in her face and her shirt is askew and it looks like she just came out of a wind tunnel. Then she kind of straightens herself out and proceeds with her line of questioning.

"You know, there are medications that can help you see things a different way."

"Um. Yeah. I know."

"You do?"

"Yeah." Sometimes I will put my hand in the denim pocket of the pillow to keep it warm. Once I found a cashew nut in there. "I do."

At this point we will both look at my folder, where it no doubt catalogs my attempts at self-medication that played no minor part in landing me here.

"That's not what I'm talking about."

"Okay."

Now it's Lane's turn to sigh and make her lips into a little line. Usually at this point she'll try a change of tactic. Either she'll simply change the subject or she'll go into hard-truth mode. This time, however, we momentarily put off the antidepressant talk for a rote conversational probe into the "incident" in the computer room last Thursday.

"I'd like to discuss what happened in the Media Center on Thursday."

Silence.

"I know that during lockdown you had ample time to think about it, so I'd like to hear your version of the events."

Silence. I squeezed the denim pillow.

"I'm sure you know this doesn't look good on your evaluation. If you refuse to talk to me about it, I certainly can't do anything for you."

I put my hands under my butt to keep them warm and let the pillow fall to the side.

"According to Mrs. Dandridge, you refused to sign an honor slip and then tried to stab her with a pen."

I start rocking back and forth. "If I had *tried* to stab her with a pen, I would have done it."

"So you didn't try to stab her."

"No. I like, fake-lunged at her and slammed my fist down on the table, and the pen still happened to be in it and it came down on her book."

Suddenly I was exhausted. It had been a while since I'd actually strung a sentence together.

"'Fake-lunged.'"

"Yeah."

"May I ask why you decided to do that?"

"Have you ever met Mrs. Dandridge?"

"I'm sure I don't have to tell you that just because you don't like someone doesn't give you permission to be violent toward them."

Permission. That's another buzzword here. Everyone talks about getting permission to do anything. I'm like, what index card do I have to sign to get permission to blow this eyelash off my sweatpants? And also: can someone just get me out of this linoleum trench and stick me in a field somewhere?

"Yeah, well, she is a dumb bitch."

"Please do not swear at me."

"It's not a swear word."

"What?"

"Bitch."

It was quiet for a moment. Lane looked down at my folder and tapped her fingers on the side of her chair. Then she leans forward and crinkles her eyes and looks into the distance. I thought she was going to start talking about my future, which she does sometimes, like, "What are you going to *do?*" As if the world is one big all-you-can-eat buffet and I just have to show up.

But this time, instead of going for some fake optimism, she goes, "I like to garden. Have you ever done any gardening—landscaping or anything?"

Silence.

"Sometimes, during the spring, I like to visit my sister in Vermont. She has a garden in the backyard and when I go up there, she always saves a patch for me, so when I visit, I can plant my mint and thyme and basil. I've been doing that for thirteen years now. I bring the herbs home later in the summer and use them, but that's a time when I can honestly say I'm happy. When I'm gardening at my sister's. Do you have anything like that, Jacob, that you can point to? A time in your life when you can say that you were happy?"

I completely ignored this question. I stared out of a window into the hallway but then realized that it might be perceived as a variety of contemplation, and I didn't want to prolong the time before her inevitable monologue about antidepressants, because then I can just tune out. Lane put her pen in her mouth and straightened out her necklace. I blew some hair out of my face. However, if I thought it would make any difference, if I thought anything I said would alter her shrink-wrapped perception of me, I might have blasted her with this memory, which has somehow managed to preserve itself in the unplugged minifridge that is my brain:

Condor Court

When me and my mom were still living in Texas, I had a best friend named Rocky (don't ask me why that was his name because I don't know, it just was). I met Rocky in our civics class in middle school. He was drawing a piranha swimming through a grid and I was like, "That. Is. Sweet."

Rocky lived in a different part of town, on a street called Falcon Avenue, in a new neighborhood called Falcon Mews. Everything in Falcon Mews was new, including the trees and the grass, which was laid down like carpet rolls and just supposed to take.

Before all the construction, it had been scrubby desert land with like, a beat-up neon baseball cap lying in the middle of it every once in a while. But now it was an empty neighborhood with huge unlocked houses and expensive specks of light wobbling on everything and this fizzy new feeling like someone had just popped the tab and let out the breath of five hundred factory couches.

Rocky's was one of the first families to move in. So after we became friends, we spent all our afternoons on the outskirts of the development wandering through the houses. It was really quiet out there, I mean like *stampeding* with quiet, except for when a truck would zoom by.

We got plenty high in rooms meant for babies and guests. We lay out like pancakes on hot driveways. We peed in shiny master bathrooms. Sometimes there was fake fruit in the kitchen if the house was meant to be displayed. Rocky stole beer from his dad and we drank it on top of a heap of pink insulation in one of the unfinished basements. We wandered around and left the doors hanging open. We threw rocks through windows. We skipped school and climbed the frames of houses that weren't done. Rocky once stepped on a nail that went almost halfway through the side of his foot and we were like, "oh, shit," but then we went back to his house and put a Band-Aid on it and it magically healed.

We had miles of carpet, acres of counters, cubic square feet of *plush;* all of it white, clean, and pristine. These people were going to be rich. Their mailboxes were shaped like their houses. Their refrigerators were roomy and assertive. And then there was the chapel-like stillness, the bought-and-paid-for prairie light traveling slowly across the counter tops.

We surfed through it, gobbled it up, and freebased the welling reflections on everything that shined.

I would never live in a place like that.

All of the streets were named after birds of prey. There was Falcon Avenue and Snowy Owl Street. Our favorite house was on Condor Court. It was bigger than the others, furnished and complete. I think it was meant to be the display house for the entire complex; even the dining room table was set for dinner. At each seat there were plates that looked like flower petals with knives and forks fanning out from them. At a side table, on a folded piece of linen, was a copper bucket filled with fake ice. And nestled into the ice, at an elegantly casual tilt, was a prop bottle of champagne.

One afternoon, we dumped the ice—warm clear plastic cubes—out in the kitchen. And it wasn't long before we proved our hypothesis: if you got enough of the ice pieces under your feet, with the right amount of propulsion, you could slide across the shiny floor with jolting, heart-slamming speed.

We pulled a couch over from the living room. And thus began one marathon afternoon where over and over again we skated the ice pieces across the kitchen, slamming into the soft lap of the couch, sometimes moving it to accommodate more advanced courses and a heightened skill level, culminating in Rocky skidding across the floor at breakneck speed, vaulting over a counter, pulling out a light fixture, and landing on the couch so hard that the whole thing tipped over backward.

Later, exhausted, we decided to go and lie down in the empty pool outside. Even though the sun was going down, it was still warm through my shirt and I felt like I was in a huge plaster palm. I wasn't really thinking about anything and when I look back, I remember that nothing was really weighing on me at that time. My eyes started to close, but before they did, I saw a shooting star, and it was like the universe was giving me a high five.

In other words, yes, I know what it's like to be happy. I've been happy before. It's like trying to pee when you're really high—sometimes it seems impossible but it's not like I don't know *how*.

Obviously I did not say any of this to Lane. We sat in silence for a while longer. I noticed the dream catchers fluttering against the bulletin board, gestured toward them, and said, "Are those supposed to be Native American?"

This time Lane did not turn around to look. She sighed. "You seem especially interested in my office this afternoon."

"It's just a question."

"It seems to me like you're avoiding the topic."

I put my hand in the jeans pocket of the denim pillow again, hoping maybe there'd be something else in there this time, like a barbecue chip or a glass eye.

More silence.

Finally Lane sat back and opened my file. She looked through a few papers, took off her glasses, and said, "A lot of the inmates here find it helpful to use medication as a way of understanding just *how* it is they're supposed to feel…"

A Typical Day

7:30. Lights come on with a hollow metallic click. Open eyes. Realize that you are once again drenched in sweat. Consider trying to salvage a moment of sleep. Let eyelids slide down. Be jolted awake by a curt knock on the door and Aaron saying, "Up...*now.*" Continue to let eyelids slide down. Be jolted awake by a harder, more personal knock on the door. "Jacob. I mean it." Peel blanket halfway off body. Peel blanket completely off body. Sit up. Pry fingers apart. Wipe nose. Touch cheek. Click jaw back and forth. Sit in a sludgy, dozing state for a while. Put hands down, feel the slippery plastic mattress beneath the top sheet. Look around. Notice the thick white paint on the walls, the frosted glass window in your heavy wooden door, the crispy smattering of bugs in the fluorescent light rod above you. Reality gurgles and slowly fills your brain: you're still here. Frantically search room for something to gouge out eyes with. Fall back onto mattress. Aaron now shoves the door open. "Jacob. Two words: pen privileges."

8:00. Find yourself standing in line in the cafeteria. Feel like something sodden and dead that has been rejuvenated by sticky electricity. Feel cold and nauseated and not at all like eating. Desean, ahead of you, pushes Eddie. Eddie whips around and looks at him with an almost grateful hatred. He's smiling as he pushes back, hard. Desean falls back into you. Aaron and Jake are suddenly there. There's some scuffling in which you get elbowed in the side.

Consider your options. Oatmeal. Cornflakes with milk that comes out of a metal teat. Some fruit. Everything is plastic, Styrofoam, portioned, cold. You consider cornflakes, but then you picture them sticking to the side of the bowl, soggy in their thin public-school milk. Settle on a bland tap-water apple.

Sit at round table. Stare at apple.

9:30. Now you're in classroom 107A, down the hallway from the cafeteria. You're sitting in a plastic chair that's stuck to the ground. You still haven't shaken the feeling of having been jostled, injected with some kind of germicide fluorescent light, slapped with a label, packaged, and then sent down the assembly line like a budget government product. You are very cold and have put your hands in your armpits which is just making your armpits cold.

Roy Hassle is at the front of the room, sitting next to the overhead projector, paging through a workbook and humming to himself. He doesn't seem to notice you are all there. He seems like he is getting sick, because he keeps sniffing and wiping his nose on his thick sweater sleeve, which looks like it was given to him by a pilgrim.

10:30. You are, unbelievably, still in classroom 107A. Hassle finally decided to give a diluted lecture on the branches of government, accompanied by a haphazardly photocopied handout. You have been dozing in and out and trying not to slip out of your chair. Your brain is a daytime television selection of rerun memories. You try to think of Chippy, her shiny, wet shoulder blades; that time her eyelashes got stuck together, and the feel of the itchy sofa, and the stereo system placed randomly in the middle of the room.

Instead, you find yourself thinking of that girl whose name may or may not be Andrea you've seen in the hallway and computer room a few times. You wonder if her name is indeed Andrea and a few other things, such as why, when you saw her standing in line two days ago, holding her wrist in between her thumb and forefinger, you felt sick to your stomach.

You look up. Hassle is doing that thing he always does, which is to pretend-search the room for someone to answer the question he just posed. His face roves around with a placid, place-keeping smile, and he knows, as we all do, that no one is going to volunteer. He looks back down at his binder and continues.

11:30. Lunch. Every food item seesaws between the two poles of taste in this cafeteria—ketchup and tepid milk. There's the faint lemon industrial cleaner smell as well. You have something on your plate that has liquid cheese on top of it and you've also opted for two tiny brownies that have both been tightly wrapped in plastic about fifty times. Across the table Jamie is sticking his straw in the same kind of liquid cheese that you have. Aaron is talking about his own juvenile delinquency, as he is wont to do, which, I don't dislike Aaron or anything. And you can tell he had some 1980s spark to be a high-fiving confidant to a bunch of troubled youths. But due to what rumor has as a failed engagement, or who knows what, the light has gone from his eyes. Sometimes he'll be sitting in his kiosk in our suite, next to the radio apparatus, staring off into the distance, and you know he's not thinking of the next watery educational activity.

You think about how you might see that girl whose name might or might not be Andrea on the way out of the cafeteria because the girls usually eat after the guys. You wonder where she's from. What she did to get in here. Why she holds her wrist like that, in between her thumb and her forefinger. Because it's not the kind of thing that's on the usual platter of human gestures, or of ways to hold yourself when you're waiting in line. You wonder, in general, if there's other stuff like that about her—things that don't make any sense but that you just *get*.

You think about what it's like in the east wing of this building, where the girls are. You know it's probably set up the same
way, with rooms around a larger common room making up the
various suites. And that they have the same series of chores that
you do. But for some reason you picture them passing around a
little medieval-looking satchel of dried flowers, holding it up to
their noses and then closing their eyes as they inhale. And then
they pick up their thin arms to do one another's hair and go
down on each other.

Aaron and Jake start rounding up forks from the various
tables. Then they stand by the trash can and go through each
of them. Because here at the JDC, everything with a sharp edge
has to be counted.

4:30. You're walking down the hallway on the way to the courtyard; being marched down a dim, cold corridor for your helping
of "outside." Even though there's nothing outsidish about the
courtyard, which is a concrete square surrounded by the building. The only natural thing is the grass bursting out of the crack
on the basketball court. Being in the courtyard relieves your
need to be outside the way drinking an inch of lukewarm water
out of a depressing plastic cup quenches your thirst.

So you're walking, staring at your shoes, and then you look up
and Pastor Todd is suddenly there. He's careening toward your
group, searching the faces of everyone in front of you because he
is the king of solicitous eye contact. It's like his eyes are two rov-
ing searchlights and no matter where you are — you can run and
try to hide in the trees or in a doghouse in someone's backyard —
you will inevitably be splashed with them; he's zeroing in on you
and flashing his hostile smile and asking why you don't come to
his Bible study elective during free time.

He has the tan, stretched face of a B-list celebrity with blown-back features like he's constantly being blasted with a jet stream of wind. He also loves Seattle, as he will tell you within the first five minutes of conversation, because apparently arbitrarily picking a city and expressing your allegiance to it counts as having a personality. I've heard he drives a Hummer and preaches out at a mega-church called Skyelm.

Before you have a chance to look away, you're locked into eye contact with him. Your group is about to pass him and his hand is up in a high-five position. He goes, "'Sup, Jake?" You stare straight ahead and keep walking. His hand hangs in the air for a second and then falls to the side. He goes, "See you tonight," with what you consider to be a touch of aggression.

You wish the girl whose name might or might not be Andrea could have seen you not high-five Pastor Todd.

5:30. Another meal, another embarrassed-looking corn dog. Then it's off to shower in the bathroom with its grid of dirty tile and shallow navels where the drains are. This place has like, industrial water pressure. You stand there and let a stream of it pummel your chest.

6:30. Cleaning time. Today you are responsible for the glass partition that separates the common room from the hallway outside. Aaron has rolled out the cleaning supplies. They are sitting on top of the filing cabinet next to the burlap couch. As you look over the dried, withered sponges and bottles of cleaning solution, you think: I cannot leave here. I am the most inside a building I've ever been. You get some stuff and take it over to the glass partition, which doesn't really need to be cleaned because someone did it yesterday. And so this whole activity is basically a colossal waste of time.

But you have to do it. Because you are one of a group of people that is funneled into one part of a building and then spread out into arbitrary chores and then funneled into a different part, as if walking from room to room pantomimed actual living.

So you are holding the sponge and looking out the glass partition that doesn't need to be cleaned into the hallway and it's cold and you're hungry because you didn't really eat anything all day and you wonder if anyone else in the world has ever felt this specific variety of unhappiness.

9:00. After cleaning time and room inspection it's free time. About fifteen minutes ago, as is your routine, you went up to Aaron, who was sitting in his kiosk. He was staring off into the distance and you had to say his name twice before he noticed you. He looks up.

"What is it, Jake?"

"Can I check out a pen?"

You sense he's about to say something, maybe about how he had to knock on your door three times this morning before you got up. But instead he sighs and goes, "Yeah, man," and checks you out a pen.

Back in your room, you fish the battered notebook out from under your bed, set it down on your lumpy pillow, page past everything you've so far cataloged and tracked. You turn to the right page and write, at the very top, "A Typical Day."

Dale County Limits, or The New Intake

There's a new guy that's folded into the rotation recently, David Keffler. He was in the courtyard yesterday. It was sunny out and we were playing a nebulous game of basketball where there were no defined teams and which had devolved into shifting alliances and random shot making. But everyone was kind of into it and not taking anything too seriously.

At one point, the ball bounces over to where this guy David is standing next to the seeping water fountain. It rolls over to like, a foot away from him. Anyone else in the world would have just instinctively picked it up and thrown it back to us. And so there was this moment, this pause where we all pantingly waited for him to do that. But he just stood there. He cocked his head a little, watching us, with this expression that struck me at the time as being one of smug curiosity. Like we were all in a Petri dish and he was waiting to see what kind of reaction would follow. Finally Eddie loped over there and got the ball. But not before saying something hassled and accusatory to David. Which caused his expression to dissolve slightly.

"Fuck is that guy?" said Eddie when he came back.

"Kensington," said Jamie Perkins.

Most of us here at the JDC come from a similar broken family/bad influence/boring afternoon background that has led to our various crimes and misdemeanors. I'd be willing to wager that our families occupy the same income bracket as well. Since, like most places, the socioeconomic hierarchy in northern Virginia plays out along county lines, that means that the bulk of us are from Dale County.

Dale County is a clammy stretch of Virginia that peters out somewhere down around Culpepper. It, technically, is in northern Virginia. But it's not the northern Virginia of freshly painted highways and wincingly bright glass buildings. It's not the northern Virginia of tailored town centers with marble walkways and aggressive-looking plants. It's a land of deserted concrete plazas, slumping strip malls, and schools with losing sports teams.

I don't know how tax delegation works—like, what counties get what—but when it comes to that all-encompassing word, *infrastructure,* with its implications of whizzing systems of opportunity and safety nets glutted with glossy pamphlets, Dale County comes up way short. And so it's pretty routine for the inmates here to be from Vines or East Potomac High School (which is where I was).

In other words, it's strange to get someone, like David, from Kensington County. But you would be able to tell, even if you didn't know where he lived, that he wasn't from Dale. He doesn't have the requisite muted swagger or hunched shoulders that most of us share which indicates a default posture of likely physical aggression. He seems kind of damp and vulnerable, like he just busted out of an eggshell.

And usually when people first get here, they float around looking stoned or dumbfounded until familiarity with the routine unlocks their normal expressions. But David never seems to laugh or react to anything that changes his catalog features. His face always seems still and empty and reminds me of a deserted playground. His dad is supposedly a major developer up in Reston.

The first time I saw David we were all on our way to the computer room. He was walking down the hallway with some sort of lawyer/rich father figure who had a ridge of water across the crotch of his slacks like he'd leaned against the sink while he was washing his hands. Jan was with them. She was saying something and David was staring straight ahead.

He always eats by himself in the cafeteria. He chews in slow motion and methodically fixes his gaze on someone so intensely that when he reaches for his milk carton he'll accidentally poke himself on the side of his face with his straw on the way to his mouth. This has made more than one person uncomfortable and already there is a small, ionic rim of hostility forming against him.

Anyway, I wouldn't give a shit or even be writing about this if he hadn't thrown my routine out of whack this afternoon and sent me down a howling tunnel of hunger.

Snack time is after class and before vocational training or electives, and it's when we all descend upon the rec room for a number of haphazardly arranged cookies. Depending on who is in charge of snack time, Aaron or Jake, the cookies will either be laid out in little rows or still partially wrapped in their trays. But no matter what the configuration, the table remains a wasteland of budget snacks. There are the rectangular, mass-produced "butter" cookies, whose logo on the packet is a little hatchback car with heavy-lidded eyes. There are the hard, round cookies with brown pellets of what I'm assuming is meant to resemble chocolate in them. There is some sort of generic Oreo. And then there is my personal favorite—the strawberry wafer.

What commences is a loosely organized feeding frenzy, in which we all stand restlessly in line waiting to get up to the table. I'm usually able to get some strawberry wafers because they're not very popular, which is lucky for me because they're the only thing that will stanch the acid hunger that has by now overtaken my stomach as I never eat anything at lunch because the food feels hostile.

But today was different. There must have been a sea change in everyone's appetites, because each time I looked at the table, the strawberry wafer row was more and more depleted. I was standing behind David. He did this annoying thing of waiting for a second when the line moved ahead, so that the gap in front of him increased, like he was just going at his own pace, like he had all the time in the world, like he was *conducting* the line. I wanted to push him.

The fewer strawberry wafers there were, the more I wanted one. I watched Jamie up ahead. He took one of each cookie and then Keith took three strawberry wafers like some sort of sultan.

Then he looked at them quizzically as if he wasn't sure they were what he wanted.

I wanted to burrow into strawberry icing. I wanted to scale a cliff of strawberry wafers. I wanted to go down on a strawberry wafer woman. All I wanted was to eat a few strawberry wafers and sit on the sofa and stare at the whiteboard in a glucose haze like I always do.

So we're finally up at the table. David is the only one in front of me. There are two wafers left. He stands there surveying the whole table as if which cookie to pick were an epic decision he's been struggling with his whole life. Finally Desean Phillips, who is behind me, goes, "What the fuck?" David's hand hovers over the wafers for a really long time, like he's trying to get them to levitate or something. Then he reaches down and takes them and proceeds to make eye contact with me, at which point his face unlocks into a look of triumph and faint disdain.

But I don't think I really cottoned onto just how creepy he is until I found myself stuck in a conference room with him during another rehabilitative attempt cooked up in the JDC's cauldron of random programs, this one called:

Victim Awareness Session

Meet Amy M. Masterson, Alumna Victim, graduated magna cum laude from the University of Having Been Raped. Majored in tired eyes with a concentration in unnerving vulnerability.

We're in a conference room. There's a drone. It's warm for once. About ten minutes ago, me, Jamie, Eddie, Desean, Keith, David, and a few other people were diverted here on our way to the courtyard. Now we're all slouched in our chairs around a long folding table. There's a whiteboard at the front of the room, and a very durable-looking office plant in the corner. I'm negotiating different chords of boredom and drowsiness, trying to arrange my body so that it siphons the maximum amount of comfort from my plastic chair, when Desean starts talking.

"You guys know about *National Geographic*?"

No one responds. Aaron looks up and then looks down and scratches something off the side of his clipboard.

Desean continues: "One time I was walking to the store and I saw a hawk swoop down and pick up a squirrel that was right in front of me. It flew away and I was like, All right, whatever, but then it flew back and dropped the squirrel onto a *different* squirrel that was in front of me."

I feel my chest begin to swell with laughter when Aaron leans forward and says, divvying out eye contact, "You guys? I mean it. I know I don't have to say this? But we're gonna keep it chill and respectful in here. I'm watchi—"

He was interrupted by Lane, who walks into the room.

She's followed by a very clean business lady wearing a decisive-looking jacket that seems to have many different panels. You can smell her perfume as she walks by, and by the efficiency of movement with which she adjusts the straps on her purse, you can tell that she might have one of those huge, bulky, bustling lady wallets. She's also wearing a laminated pass around her neck indicating that she's a guest speaker, which she holds in place with one hand as if she was afraid it was going to wildly swing around.

Lane pulls out two chairs and they both sit. The lady puts her purse down, flicks something off her skirt, and then arranges her hands in her lap. Lane leans over and whispers something and the lady looks at her and nods vigorously.

"As you all know," says Lane, facing us, "part of your sentence is participating in a victim-awareness session." (I didn't know that.) "This is Amy Masterson."

Lane licks her thumb and quickly pages through some papers on her clipboard. She glares at Aaron. He jolts up, looks around, and gives her a sort of miniature hassled shrug. They both seem to call off whatever eye-contact dialogue they were having. Aaron sits back. Lane clears her throat.

"She's been with the program for a while. She's been kind enough to come here and talk with us about a very traumatic experience... which can't be easy." She smiles at the guest speaker, who is still staring into the distance. Lane shifts gears.

"Part of the rehabilitative process is being able to look at a situation from different angles. Being able to see something from someone else's point of view, which is something that we all—I know I do—have the ability to ignore..." She runs out of steam. "Compassion," she says. "*Empathy*.

"Here." She unclips a small stack of papers from her clipboard and hands them to Aaron, who hands a section to each of us, and that's when I find myself with yet another haphazardly photocopied handout in my possession.

"I don't have page two," says Eddie.

"What?" Lane looks up.

"Me neither," says Jamie. "And mine's damp."

"It's not *damp*," says Aaron.

"Okay," says Lane. She looks quickly at the lady and then at her watch and then at us. "We'll go over these later. But right now I'm going to go ahead and give Amy a chance to talk. And I know that she'll be impressed by how respectful we all are here at Braddock County."

Lane sits down. We all look at the lady.

She takes off her jacket and slings it over the back of her chair. There is some hair falling out of her ponytail and she now seems to possess the aloof nonchalance of someone's hot older sister. She's really pretty, like babysitter pretty. And something about the way she holds the strap of her guest pass at her neck gives me an understanding of a larger spectrum of her movements. I picture her shaking a lightbulb next to her ear.

Everyone was avoiding eye contact except for David. He was sitting completely still, with his hands crossed on the table, and was looking at her with syrupy amusement—the way you might at a child who's bumbling through the spelling of a long word.

The lady clears her throat. "Yes," she says in a not unfriendly tone. She's now straightening out her shirt in a series of dogged little gestures. "I've been doing this program for a while now. Six years, I think." She looks at her name on her guest pass. Or maybe she was just staring at the pass. "I mean, obviously, I wish I'd never *heard* of this program. But here I am." She laughs a little.

"I think it's important, definitely," she says while surveying the room. "And I also want to say that I'm not here to *accuse* you. This isn't about accu*sation*. It's about understanding violence, and about what really happens when a violent crime is committed against an innocent person . . . a random person." She continues motioning with her hand even after she's stopped talking.

She clears her throat. "About six years ago I was raped."

Now I picture her carefully scraping out the bottom of a yogurt cup, holding the spoon midair, and staring blankly into the distance.

My body felt like it was arranged all wrong. Aaron had said something about this victim awareness session a few times and I'd never paid attention. I didn't know we were going to be in the same room as a person who'd experienced something that, like, would happen to a medieval woman while her Viking village was being ravaged. An actual raped person. She was a pillaged field with a guest pass. I didn't know in which direction to look.

The lady reached up to straighten her ponytail, and when she did, some of the skin on the bottom of her arm jiggled, which made me feel, suddenly and inexplicably, bulldozed with guilt.

Unlike the crimes of a few people in the room (cough Jamie Perkins cough), mine was basically just a hassle and definitely not on the sexual abuse spectrum. But I mean, it's not like I *haven't* been angry enough to see the world as something clamped and unyielding before, beyond which, if I could just pry it open, was some lounge of exclusivity, because I totally have. But I guess there was no ponytailed portal walking around at the wrong time and wrong place next to me when I've been feeling that way. I don't know if I would ever actually do something like that.

Everyone had reached a new pitch of fidgeting. Jamie was riffling through his hair like someone had dumped a bunch of pencil shavings in it and he was trying to get them out. Desean kept yawning. Eddie was furiously scratching at something on the desk. I was rocking back and forth with my hands in my armpits.

Then there was David.

Completely still. Calmer than a lake in a movie that someone has just emptied a toxin into, with the faintest smile tugging at his lips. The lady looked around the room and I could have sworn that she snagged on him. I wanted to throw a stapler at his face.

"I'm not going to get into the details of that night," said the lady. She was playing with one of the buttons on her shirt with one hand and motioning with the other. She sat up straight. "I will say that it was completely random. A stranger. I will also say the levels of pain and fear I felt that night, I didn't think they were possible. I mean, you hear about this stuff on TV, you read about it...let's just say that I was hurt. Very, really, mortally, badly *hurt*."

She looked like she was doing a math equation in her head. "Think about it this way. Imagine you're in a house, and you've walked around in the house, and you know all of the different rooms and the whole layout. You're pretty comfortable in the house because you know where everything is. Then imagine if one day, you find out that there's a whole other room you didn't know about. That this whole time you'd been living there it existed and you just didn't know about it. That's what it was like, being attacked like that, and afterward. I had no idea that it was possible for a human being to feel that way. But it happens all the time..." She trailed off as she looked around at us.

She started and then stopped. "Think of me," she said, "riding down a hundred floors in an elevator..." She changed her mind. "I'm in front of a glass case..." She changed her mind again. "When something like that happens to you, it doesn't end the minute you wake up in a hospital, if you're lucky enough to wake up. In fact, that's just the beginning."

There was a faint line, along her neck, where her makeup ended and the real color of her skin began.

"You ever get a song stuck in your head? What if, instead of a song replaying over and over again, it was the sound of your own voice? But it doesn't even sound like you, so that when you hear it, there's always a moment when you think, who is that? What if it lasted for years? What I'm saying is"—she let go of the pass and held one of her hands with the other—"you have to relive the experience over and over again. For the doctor, for the detective..."

I looked over at David and immediately felt sick. He was now staring at the lady with a wide, frozen clown smile. It was like his lips were on a loom, stretching all the way and threatening to split. His whole face was rearranged to accommodate this pinball smile. But it wasn't actually a smile. It was more like his lips were being tuned to the highest frequency of hatred. I had to look away and then back to make sure I was seeing right.

Aaron had obviously noticed. He was staring at Lane, who was looking back and forth between David and the lady with confusion and possibly panic. Amy was still talking. She was saying, "There is no amount of—" And then she stopped when she saw him. She put her hand around her guest pass, turned to someone else, and continued. "There is no amount of counseling that can take the experience away."

Lane hefted her weight forward like she was about to get up, when David's features deflated. It was so quick, and he looked so normal, that it was like it had never happened. Even now as I'm writing this I feel like maybe I imagined the whole thing. But I know I didn't. I remember it—him sitting there, completely still, crossing so many tiny boundaries; his face drifting and drifting until it was unrecognizable.

Writing about it now, I can't figure out how big of a deal it was. Or if it was really the way I was picturing it. And I can't figure out what David was *doing*.

His face was so raw with his lips curling and his insides spilling out that there was something genital about it. He was exposing himself, but only for a moment, because then it was over and everything went on as usual. Right before anything happened, he pulled the plug, and there wasn't any flicker in his expression that indicated he thought he was going to get caught.

I can't picture anyone else here doing something like that. But David, he has this like, air-conditioned aggression that's more state-of-the-art than anyone else's.

Back in the conference room, I kept glancing at him. Now he looked withdrawn and placid, staring down at the table.

Amy kept talking, seeming intermittently strong and sad. I might have just been imagining it, but I could have sworn she was avoiding David's end of the room. She motioned more with her hands and mentioned some statistics. She talked about how she moved to a different city. I was left with the resounding feeling that I would not like to be raped.

"The person who did that to me was never caught," she said. She seemed exhausted. "I often think of what I would say to him if I ever saw him. I've thought about it a lot. And I finally figured out what it would be. I would tell him that I like the smell of hardware stores. I know it's strange, but it's just something about me. I've always liked the smell of hardware stores."

Family Day

There is only one thing that a little city of plastic cups set up on a folding table can mean, and that is that some sort of boring function is about to take place. Maybe it's the commemoration of a lesser-known holiday, or perhaps the honoring of an employee who has gone the extra mile. But here at the JDC, today, it meant only one thing: Family Day.

Family Day is when the disparate elements of our broken families collect here at the JDC in a veritable *Who's Who* of the Braddock County welfare set. I had known about Family Day for a while but had folded the idea of it into a paper airplane that had spiraled happily into the ether of my brain until I received a letter from my mother saying she was going to attend.

Upon receiving the letter I experienced a number of different feelings. It started with surprise that she owned envelopes, burgeoned into unexpected affection ringed with guilt, blew up into full-scale resentment, and then tapered off into grudging obligation.

I ended up throwing the letter away and trying not to think about it until I had to. When the day finally arrived, I repaired to the cafeteria fully expecting her to not show up. I was wrong. A look around the cafeteria revealed that other people's parents showed up, too. Eddie was sitting in silence with a morbidly obese woman in sweats. Desean was with a man who had wet-looking hair and a briefcase. David Keffler was sitting with a person who appeared to be part of the marble-pen-holding variety of wealthy father or lawyer.

Then there was my mom, standing next to the punch table with a huge tote bag. I almost didn't recognize her.

Up until the age of ten I thought my mother's name was Beans, which it isn't. It's Erin. Beans is a nickname that she forces on practically everyone she meets. High school dropout-cum-alcoholic, Erin deserves some credit for running away from an abusive home at the age of sixteen—yet one might question her judgment for shacking up with a leathery Hawaiian shirt–wearing "producer" fifteen years her senior. This was Malibu Mike. As far as I know, the only thing he ever produced was a dented car door with a bulging cartoon stingray on it smoking a cigar, which we still have, leaning against a wall in our house with some fake fish netting slung over it. One night he was doing some impromptu stand-up at a beach hotel bar when someone asked him to be in a commercial for a nearby surf shop, which he accepted, and that's where he met my mom.

Emboldened by whatever shreds of glamour she detected on local celebrity Malibu Mike, my mom decided to try her hand at modeling. Her efforts didn't yield much until she landed a spot in a local newsletter called the *MangoTown Telegraph*. This is what constituted (according to her many drunken, gravelly monologues) the apex of my mother's life. Every once in a while she'll still withdraw the crinkled edition from some drawer, which displays her in a bikini in someone's backyard and says, "Offbeat local gal loves our grills."

I believe it was in year five of their relationship that Malibu Mike became "a grouch," and landed her a bunch of times in the hospital with various concussions and broken bones. I've never seen him, except in a dusty photograph, sitting around a plastic table with some overly tan women in a beach setting. He's leaning back and pantomiming the strumming of a tiny imaginary guitar against his chest. He is also, incidentally, my father.

Left with nothing and a baby, my mother started depending on a string of abusive men who all, in a sick yet predictable pattern, resembled her father and Malibu Mike, and who all left her as she stumbled up the East Coast to here, back where she started. It was around then that she met the grunting refrigerator of a man that the state now legally recognizes as my guardian.

It's a very typical and worn-out American story. In this particular version, however, there's no redemption at the end when the protagonist goes home and learns carpentry or whatever. No, my mother is still an alcoholic who nods off every day at noon on a lipstick-stained couch. And she's still with Refrigerator Man.

The fact that my mother even knew about Family Day suggested an uncharacteristic degree of lucidity I was suspicious of even before she showed up completely clean and sober. I don't know what I expected, but I didn't expect her to show up looking like a "nice mom."

Her fingernails were newly painted with little black top hats on each of them. She was wearing a button-down shirt tucked into jeans, with an embroidered pelican coming out of the breast pocket. And she smelled like air freshener. It threw me off and I found myself wishing she would go back to her usual blurry self.

On the wall behind the table with the cups was a taped-up computer printout that said, "Welcome Families!" It had a little clip-art graphic of a picnic basket on it as if we were in some sunny field and not in the fluorescent-lit valve of a Braddock County Court subdivision.

We sat down and she asked me if I wanted anything from the vending machine and I said no. She started rummaging around in her huge tote bag for change, then she asked me again if I wanted anything and again I said no. She got up, went to the vending machine, and got herself a packet of minicookies, which she couldn't open when she got back. Then, in perhaps the first conciliatory gesture toward my mother in maybe three years, I yanked the packet away from her, rolled my eyes, opened it, and gave it back. This embarrassed both of us and for a while we were quiet.

She craned around and looked over her shoulder. I put my hands in my armpits to keep them warm. She turned back to me and drilled her fingernails on the table. I sighed and started tapping my foot. She goes, "Ow!" and her hands shot up to her ear where she readjusted an earring. We made eye contact and then both looked quickly away. I literally heard the clock ticking, as there is a big, bulky clock in the cafeteria above the serving station. I was considering the permutations of why or why not I should get some punch when someone yelled, *"You can't!"*

We all turned to stare at the morbidly obese woman sitting across from Eddie. She had some strands of hair stuck across her face and her arms were pooling on the table in front of her. Eddie glanced around and then cracked his knuckles, sat forward, and hissed something at her.

I looked back at my mom. She was slumped over and staring into the distance. I go, "How are the cookies?"

She turned to me and brightened. "They're great, hon!" She held up the packet and pointed at something on it with one of her shiny fingernails. "They go with my diet." Staring out from the corner of the packet was a woman with big hair and a frank expression. Right next to her it said, "Part of the *Contours* meal plan!"

"So it's like a tie-in?" I said.

"What?"

"A tie-in."

"What's that?"

"I don't know. Never mind."

"I got a job," said my mom. Her eyes darted searchingly around my face.

I looked away. Someone, somewhere, coughed. I watched as one side of the "Welcome Families!" printout became unstuck and floated down the wall, the whole thing now hanging by a single piece of tape.

This is me yawning and fake-stretching, as if by clinging to some tempo of regular gestures I will be able to avoid looking at my mom's face, which will be a broken picture frame of anxiety. This is me in my role of expression control — because my mom is someone who can't divorce her facial expression from how she's feeling inside; such as when she's channeling deep despair, or worse, when she's channeling deep despair but is trying to hide it, in which case she'll enact this kind of belly-flopping airplane of a smile. The lights in the ceiling flickered. Someone accidentally knocked over a tower of plastic cups. This is me looking around hurriedly, still avoiding her eyes and saying, in order to pave the way for a normal conversation, under the assumption that it's even possible for my mom to hold a job amid her daily alcoholic waltz, "You did?"

"Yeah," she said, relieved. "It's at a great new place, in Greenpond? You know the shopping center? It's at a salon called New

Attitudes. I wash people's hair." She touched her own hair. Someone behind me pushed their chair out with a loud screech. I looked over at David Keffler. The man sitting across from him was riffling through a briefcase and had a moat of white hair around an otherwise bald head.

My mom broke a cookie in half and tried to dislocate a chocolate chip from its socket. "You know," she said, her voice lit like a car show with forced humor, "that old microwave is still mad at me."

I pictured our kitchen with its warped linoleum floor and empty cabinets, the torn window screen. There's a big microwave hanging down above the oven. It has wood-paneled sides and huge orange digital numbers, and if you don't press the right configuration of dusty buttons it makes a series of accusatory beeps. This is a problem for my mom, for whom the microwave is the main culinary tool. She always claims it's mad at her when she has trouble heating one of her compartmentalized meals.

"It's not mad at you," I said. "You're probably just not doing it right."

"But I always do it exactly how you said." She brushed some crumbs off the table into her cupped hand and then didn't have anywhere to throw them out and so put them back on the table. "I press defrost and then the number of minutes I want it to cook for and then I press the start button."

"You're not supposed to press defrost," I said, picturing her jabbing the button pad. "You just press how long you want it to cook for."

"But what if I want it to defrost?"

"It'll defrost when it cooks."

"Well, then why is there a button that says defrost?" She said *defrost* with a hassled-sounding southern accent.

"I don't know."

"I'll never figure it out," she said distractedly, looking into the distance.

Someone's cell phone rang. I saw the man across from David patting around his shirt and pants.

"But what about you, hon?" said my mom. She sat forward. "How do you like this place?" She looked around. "Are you making friends?"

"I dunno," I said, shrugging.

"They treat you okay?"

"No."

"How's the food?"

"Stupid."

"What do you do all day?"

"Nothing."

I could see her getting anxious. She played with an earring. She stared down at her packet of cookies and mouthed the words *perfect for dipping.*

I put one of my hands on the table in front of me and then placed the other one on top and said, "How's the Ford?"

"Oh, fine," she said. She ate the last cookie and looked around thoughtfully. "Well, the timing belt needs to be replaced. I don't even know what that is. I just know it costs money."

"It times the sparks that cause the mini-explosions that make your car move," I said. "Or something like that."

"Yeah," she said. "That sounds about like what they said."

I looked up to see the man across from David get up and walk quickly to the punch table. He stood there staring at the plastic cups.

My mom started talking as if she'd just remembered something. "This woman came up to me at the mini-mart the other day. She said she knew you."

"What?"

"A teacher or something. I was trying to buy garbage bags."

"Who was it?"

"She said she had taken a special interest in you." My mom was motioning with her hands now. "Fray? Frapp? She said she took a special interest in you. She was stressing me out, talking at me..."

There was a viscousy reflection of light on the vending machine behind the snack table. I stared at that as I tried to remember. Mrs. Frye. She was my sixth-grade history teacher. She had given me a list of books she wanted me to read. She sometimes wore an apron to class and had big thick knuckles.

"She kept asking me about you, and I didn't know what to say," said my mom, agitated. She rummaged around in her tote bag and withdrew a pack of cigarettes.

I said, "I don't think you can—"

"She wouldn't leave me alone. I smiled at her, I said 'how-de-do,' and she kept asking me questions."

My mom put a cigarette in her mouth and it bobbed up and down as she kept talking.

"Kept saying about a project you worked on. Something about the Middle Ages, or the Dark Ages, or medieval times..."

She stared at me and patted the table in front of her, feeling for a lighter. Then she looked down and started rummaging through her bag again.

"And about how you made something, or you did something special with it that she remembered, something you did at home..."

My mom was getting more and more agitated as she rummared through her bag. She kept taking things out, slamming them on the table, and putting them back in—her keys, a bottle of hand moisturizer, a heavy glass salt shaker.

"She said she always remembered it because it was so great. Something about a kind of paper . . ."

"Parchment." I said.

"What?" She stopped, took the cigarette out of her mouth, and looked at me.

"Parchment paper." I put my hands in my armpits. "I poured lemon juice on the paper and held it over the toaster so it burned a little and became brown and so it was like my report on the Middle Ages was written on parchment paper."

She sighed and let her hands collapse over her bag. Something seemed to register with her from far away. I looked down at the table. I hadn't thought of that project in a really long time.

"They told me they wanted to put you in these classes," she said. Her eyes, which were becoming glassy, settled on something beyond me. "And then they looked at me in this *way*.

"All of this," she said, swirling her hands around to indicate everything. "All of this . . ."

We sat there. I was sort of stunned. It might have been the first time since I was a kid that I'd seen her consciousness bubble up to the surface of reality enough to actually begin some sober analysis of a situation. But she didn't finish.

"So . . . you're going to get it fixed?" I said.

"What?"

"The timing belt."

"Oh, yeah. Soon as I find a way to pay for it."

My mom crinkled up the bag of cookies into a wad and then reopened it and squinted her eyes at it as if it were a map.

"Steve," she said, "says hello."

And with that, whatever kindling camaraderie we'd been able to gather during the past twenty minutes was blown away. I felt cold. Steve is my mom's name for Refrigerator Man.

Refrigerator Man

I've known him since I was twelve years old. And ever since the day I met him, since the day he came slamming into our house at four in the morning with my mom and shoved his massive hairy elbows onto the kitchen table—which is where he decided to stay for the next five years—I have been continually awestruck by how much of a dick he is.

I don't know that much about his past, despite the fact that he's been living with us, on and off, for almost six years. I do know that he's got an ex-wife named Sandy who he sometimes confuses with my mom as in, "Sandy! What! I mean Beans, go blow into the VCR player!"

He is, by trade, an electrician, specializing in refrigerator repair. But he also resembles a refrigerator in his hulking, unhinged way. I don't want to give the wrong impression by saying he's an electrician, however, if that implies he has a steady job or even gets up at the same time every day. I can count on my fingers the few periods during which he's actually gone to work, periods that coincide with his short-lived moments of professed sobriety.

But he's always drunk. He blindly rolls through the house until he can find whatever sofa, kitchen chair, or inflatable pool raft (we don't have a pool, I don't know where we got that thing) to contain him. At which point he will continue whatever drink he was nursing and shout out random orders to whoever is within earshot.

He has the anger and sense of entitlement of a Vietnam vet except without the traumatic combat experience to explain it. His answer to everything is to pound it into submission until it goes away. I have a chipped canine from when he threw an enamel hand mirror at my face when I accidentally crossed his line of vision. I won't go into what he's done to my mom. Needless to say, she won't be relinquishing her heavy-duty concealer anytime soon.

It started pretty much the day he moved in with us. As soon as he made himself comfortable, he started dealing out punches like we lived in some sort of abuse casino. I wasn't around much, but when I was, he treated me like a piece of furniture he had to shove aside whenever he was rumbling through the hallway. He treated Beans alternately as a little girl, rocking her back and forth on his knee and pushing her hair behind her ears, and as a hovering, clothes-wearing fly that he had to swat every once in a while.

But the absolute worst thing about Refrigerator Man is that he could sometimes be all right. There were months when things were sort of normal and he didn't fly into any dislocating rages. When a fatherly instinct might take hold and his face would splinter into something resembling a smile and he'd be like, "Jake, man. Why don't you get the chain saw from the garage and we'll cut down that tree together." Or he'd come home from work with actual groceries and cook a steak while Beans hung around and made jokes and didn't look as tired as usual.

It was never long, though, before he went back to being himself. I came home really late one night to find him and Beans sitting at the kitchen table. Except Beans was flopped over on top of it, her head turned to one side. Her nose was bleeding. I couldn't tell if she was okay or not. Refrigerator Man was smoking. There was an overturned can of beer on the table with the puddle seeping into my mom's hair. He just sat there over her, not moving it. And for some reason that made me angrier than any of the times he'd hit me or her.

So I swung my backpack at him. And whatever was in it,

some batteries and a key chain, burst out and bounced off his face and he didn't even change expressions. He sat there like a flannel mountain in a chair. I went for him, trying to punch him in the face. I put all of my weight into it. I coughed and yelled a lot. And then he had me pinned down, holding my wrists together behind my back. Then he let me go and I went for him again, and he pinned me down again. After it happened a third time, I pushed over the kitchen table, which finally woke Beans up, and ran out of the house.

I hate him. My anger is wide and nuanced. It is gaping and ancient. It's stronger than when you're in the ocean and a wave pulls you down and you get a sense of some gravitational hinge powering things. It is stronger than that. It is all-encompassing and more glinty than five hundred suburban pools at midday.

So back in the cafeteria, we're still sitting there, and my mom is squinting at me. I've completely closed down. She's dumbfounded, confused as to what could have possibly caused this change in our meeting. She looks up into the air, suddenly possessed, and jerks her head around as if she's following a dizzy gnat with her eyes.

People around us are getting up and throwing their cups away. Officer O'Connell is at the door with Aaron and Jake, waiting to escort us back to our rooms. There are the final shuffling noises of everyone getting ready to go. My mom says hopefully, "It's been quiet around the house without you. I know you were never home much, but now that you're gone, I notice it more." Whatever the fuck that means. She picks up the wadded cookie bag and her pack of cigarettes and puts them in her bag. We walk out together. Before she turns around to walk the other way down the hall, along with the other parents or relatives, she lightly touches my shoulder.

In Which I Make Eye Contact and Break Conversational Ground with a Girl Whose Name Can Now Be Confirmed as Andrea

So last Thursday in the computer room this girl knocked over the tin of pens on Mrs. Dandridge's desk and they fell to the floor with a metallic crash that jerked everyone's head around to look. It was Andrea. Okay. Every time I see her I notice something different. For instance: this time I noticed that when her hair is pulled back, there are little tufts that fall in front of her ears. And suddenly I felt that the universe was being revealed to me like a kitten's belly under its pried-open paws.

We don't interact with the girls here very much. Sometimes in the computer room and sometimes during movie nights in the rec room. But it doesn't really matter because even when there are girls around, you can't follow any thought avenues to their logical conclusion because there's always someone like Mrs. Dandridge patrolling, who, one look from her and your boner basically turns inside out and goes up inside you and you actually *become* a girl. Which was really hard when Kelly Feldman was around, who was like, a way-too-early-developed 110-pound Popsicle that you just wanted to melt all over your hand.

Every once in a while I'll be unintentionally attracted to Denise Henly. She's got this whole lip ring scar, short greasy hair, psychotic-abandonment thing going on that makes me think she would give really energetic blow jobs. The girl I was seeing before I came here was named Chippy, and she had really pretty skin, except for a huge train-track scar on her chest running up and down between her tits. She was always really distracted because she had to take care of two blank-eyed little brothers.

I think about her sometimes and wonder how she's doing. Whenever we would do it I got the feeling she was leaving bread crumbs behind so that she could find her way back.

1st time having sex: I was fourteen and we were living in a trailer and one of my mom's leathery friends, "Diane," lifted herself on top of me. There was a loud metallic drip coming from the tap in the kitchen nook that was about a foot away. I just kind of focused on that.

1st hand job: Erica Topochek, at my friend Kyle's house when I was fifteen at a party. We were on his parents' water bed and they walked in on us. Incidentally, that is also the first time I noticed that adults' faces can hold many different expressions at once.

1st blow job: Jen Fletcher, at a different party at Kyle's house. This time it was in the shower. Jen kept on looking up at me and getting water in her eyes. She employed a sponge that was shaped like a seashell.

1st girlfriend: Amy Valdiverre. We talked a lot on her bunk bed and stared at the tie-dyed sheet she had tacked to her ceiling. Being with Amy was like rolling down the side of a hot grassy hill on a pretty good day. She ended up moving to San Dimas, California.

1st girl who ever made me feel like crap: Amy Valdiverre. Her parents were real-estate agents, and she moved to California and never wrote or called or anything like she promised she would. For about a year I felt about as good as the twitching wires in the neck of a decapitated cyborg.

1st girl who liked me so much I could tell I could do whatever I wanted to her: Grace Owen. I think I was the first guy she ever kissed or did anything with. She had straight blond hair that would make a sort of hallway to her face when she tipped her head forward.

1st time I had sex where afterward I was so depressed I wanted to die: With one of my foster moms, Mrs. Kelly ("Call me Janice"). One afternoon she asked me to put a disk into the DVD player and then came up behind me and put her hands on my stomach and we fucked. I was banging her up against their crappy entertainment center, looking at a card tacked to the wall that said something about being over the hill. There were all of these despotic scented plug-ins around the house. That night I sat in my designated room, under a storm cloud of peach, and felt like crying.

Here is something about the girls here: Most of them were molested and are lashing out at some composite deadbeat dad and you don't want to mess with that.

Here is something about girls in general: You'll be lying there next to them watching all these emotions ripple across their face and you can never be sure what kind of weird or desperate thing they're going to say next.

Here is something else about girls in general: It is easy to get them to want you when you know what to do. All you have to do is pretend, in every separate moment, that you're wrapped up in something else that is really important. Like there's some hostage crisis in your head and you're totally on the ball about it and walking around purposefully and squinting up at the guard tower while coordinating this whole caper and so you don't really have time for anything else, especially not the girl who is by now looking at you with her swampy, malleable eyes. And then it's like, welcome to the land of falling hair and damp mouths and shoulder blades that look like sand dunes. It's like, right this way down the hand-job hallway to the blow-job seminar room and the conference center of little patterned motions that make everything wet.

It goes without saying that this juvenile detention center represents a sharp downturn in my bed tourism. The only things to supplement my substantial but fading memory bank of porn are the STD pamphlets in the rec room, which, if you erase the sores with your imagination, yield some pretty realistic poon.

Then there's Andrea. Once I got out of the initial haze of being here, I immediately noticed her. The first time I saw her was at one of our enforced "socials" in the cafeteria. Everyone else was standing in one of several clumps at various points around the room, but she was by herself, next to a huge trash can. Upon seeing her face, I had the feeling that I'd seen her somewhere before. It was a sudden and unexpected sensation, like someone tapped my brain on the shoulder. We made eye contact. She looked quickly away.

I was standing with Eddie and Desean. Eddie had made a gun out of his thumb and pointer finger and was shooting the ground, and Desean was dancing around the bullets. I pretended I needed to go to the bathroom. As I walked across the cafeteria I looked at her again. She was bobbing up and down on her feet. She checked her wrist as if to find out the time even though she wasn't wearing a watch. Then she noticed something out of the ordinary on her hand and started inspecting it. The way she was standing, with her head tilted and her wrist held midair, and her stillness like she was petrified in sudden thought made me feel like I'd been punched in the stomach.

I spent the last twenty minutes of the social shredding a napkin I'd gotten from the games table.

That was about three weeks ago. Since then I've seen her every three or four days, in the courtyard when our rotation matches up, or in the computer room. Each time it's like the sighting of a rare bird. I feel disoriented and have the instinct to pat myself down to make sure I *have* everything.

Thursday, however, in the computer room was the first time I got to see her up close. She knocks over the aforementioned tin of pens. It makes this huge apocalyptic clatter. Everyone jerks their head around to look and then goes back to work but I keep watching. She collects the pens and throws them back into the tin like each one is a separate little javelin. *Ping! Ping! Ping!* Her hair is tied back except for these feathery wisps falling out, and I now notice that she has like, graceful Victorian-lady fingers. Mrs. Dandridge is really annoyed, holding her paperback to her chest and trying to peer over the desk without getting up.

There's one more pen under the desk and she reaches for it, then pauses for just a second, withdraws, and leaves it there. She gets up and smacks the tin down on the desk with an amount of force that could be interpreted as insolent. Mrs. Dandridge looks like she's not quite sure how to react to this. She straightens out some sort of lacy attachment to the front of her blouse and says, "Is that *all* of them?" Andrea starts restlessly tapping her foot and nods her head. Mrs. Dandridge says, with extra-concentrated condescension, "Fine. Would you mind actually signing one of *these?*" She nudges an honor slip forward on the desk.

I'm sitting at computer number three, toward the front of the room, and I'm about five feet away from her. I can see a ridge across the front of her T-shirt, a tiny step in the material, that would indicate a bra. I wonder if she wears one of those weird linebacker padded bras. Or maybe it's lace. Or maybe it's like a gauzy, thin, slightly stretched cotton mound.

At this point I turn back to my computer because it started to seem weird that I was all turned around to watch. A quiet tedium settles around me. I wrestle with myself not to look at the sneering clock at the front of the room. Andrea enters my peripheral vision. She walks up my side of the room and has lost whatever swagger she had in front of Mrs. Dandridge as she glances around nervously for a computer. She finally sits at the computer in front of me and places her fingers gingerly on the keyboard as if she's never seen one before. But before she did that, she looked back in my direction and we made eye contact for a moment. Things I notice: she has really red lips that give her face a smeared sort of prettiness. Her body: nice proportions, like everything is the perfect quivering cupful.

But I'm getting ahead of myself. Because the thing is I actually talked to her, yesterday, at the social:

Oh, What a (Boring) Night

Every once in a while the JDC puts on a social. These are drug-free, alcohol-free, and fun-free events in the cafeteria, where the nurses set up a few bowls of Doritos and call it a day. We're meant to shuffle around in our sweats and hopefully socialize with one another, or indulge in one of the two board games that will be laid out on a table. Despite the efforts of the nurses, these events rarely yield the kind of sweaty, revelatory moments that usually constitute what most people consider to be a good time. Therefore, they're bleak and depressing and no one would go to them if they weren't, in fact, mandatory.

Last night was one such social. It was a time for gathering

under the dimmed cafeteria lights. A time for holding plastic cups filled with soda and looking out of the cafeteria windows and into the hallway. A time for not playing the board games that were on one of the tables. A time for wondering what time it was, but most of all, it was a time for snacks. The folding tables were dressed with paper tablecloths on top of which was a sparkling spectrum of sodas—matched only by a tempting array of party mixes whose zesty hues and bite-size nature could only serve to promote a sense of fun.

However, it was the details that completed the night: the circular formation of napkins on the table, the five balloons idling in the corner, and of course, Officer O'Connell, who was kind enough to attend in full police regalia.

Jamie Perkins got things going with a number of inappropriate gestures aimed at Nurse Feingard. At one point he had her pinned against the cafeteria wall and was hissing what I can only imagine were sweet nothings in her ear as she flailed her arms around. Officer O'Connell then took it upon himself to cut in, handcuff Jamie, and escort him back to his room.

It was only after I went back to pounding cups of soda that I noticed Andrea standing next to a bowl of Cheezums. I went over to the other end of the snack table to throw away my cup in one of the many huge trash cans and looked at her again. Her hair was down this time. She was standing with her arms crossed in that insecure girl way and also appeared to have some sort of blushing disorder where there were clouds of red wandering across her face.

I was doing these insane equations in my head, weighing the proportions of how much effort it would be to actually talk to her versus the probability of us ever doing it, when she "pretended" to need another cup of soda and came over to where I was standing, which was basically like hoisting up a huge neon sign saying she wanted to go down on me. So I decided to take the cue and said, "You were in the computer room last Thursday."

She looked at me quickly and goes, "Um. Yeah."

"You knocked over that tin of pens."

She goes, "Yup. That was me." Which didn't exactly lube up the way for further conversation. So I said, "Cool," and then looked around.

Pastor Todd was doing his usual thing of going up to people and creeping them out with his scalding enthusiasm. Officer O'Connell was back in the corner, watching everyone and shifting his weight from one leg to the other. Aaron and Jake were talking by a stack of folding chairs. I looked back at Andrea, who was sorting through the Cheezums and was about to turn around and walk away, when she goes, "I like your shirt." Which, ha-ha, we all wear the same shirts, but it wasn't the least funny thing someone could have said and I also figured it was maybe a toe test into the kind of sarcasm that I basically consider to be my calling card.

So I said, "Thanks, they're sweeping the nation." And she laughed quickly and brushed her hair away from her cheek like a sort of petulant little girl and I wondered if she was going to be one of those girls who was sexy because she was sort of childish or sexy because she was sort of knowing and sophisticated. Either way I wanted to bone her.

She goes, "I'm Andrea."

I go, "I'm Jacob."

And I guess that could be pretty much the start to any conversation that could ever possibly happen in the world, except when you're here at the JDC, there's one question that kind of anchors everything when you first meet someone. It's the topic we all have in common and it's the thing that Andrea brought up as she slammed some Cheezums into her mouth with her palm, which was:

What Did You Do?

The reasons most of us have ended up here are varied and many and create a colorful tapestry of amateur crime. There's armed robbery, manslaughter, aiding and abetting, drinking and driving, sexual assault, regular assault. You've got your sister rapers, mother beaters, pipe-bomb makers. We're not really encouraged to talk about our previous infractions. But everybody does; everybody finds out what everybody did sooner or later.

Most of us are here on drug-related charges. The procurement of, the imbibing of, disseminating of, and actions committed while on. Jamie Perkins, for instance, while not a direct perpetrator, was present at last fall's much-publicized murder, execution-style, of three people in the parking lot of West Springfield High in the midst of a cocaine transaction gone wrong. During a meth binge Eddie Alvarez assaulted a grocery store clerk getting off a late shift. And Wesley Burlin supplied half of George Mason University's freshman population with enough Adderal to finish finals two years in a row.

Then there are the deep-seated behavioral cases like Keith Meyers, who beat up and then tried to have sex with his sister. And Dwayne Knots, who like, poisoned a bear or something, I don't even know. The only person whose crime is a complete mystery is David Keffler. He doesn't talk to anyone, so no one's had a chance to ask him. I doubt it was some desperate in-the-moment thing, though. It was probably calculated and super-fucked-up because I'm no clinical psychologist but I can tell that guy has got some rage.

As for me, what I did was simple enough. Nothing quirky or diabolical. I didn't do anything sweeping like corral a bunch of single moms into a boardroom and then gas it. I didn't realign the universe so all the planets crashed into one another and the stars got swept up like a tablecloth and all the skin got sucked off our faces. I didn't make everyone watch while I transported a graceful, mythical beast from back in time and then set it on fire.

What I'm guilty of is a pretty standard, run-of-the-mill armed robbery. More American than grass stains and painted curbs, with a little brutality thrown in for good measure.

So I was like, "Armed robbery. What about you?" Turns out Andrea was found behind Weatherford Elementary with an ounce of marijuana during recess.

"You were selling weed to ten-year-olds?"

She slammed another Cheezum into her mouth and goes, "It wasn't the best time in my life."

"Did you actually sell any?"

"Sure."

"So you were like, crouching in the shade by the bike racks or something?"

"Yes and no," she said.

"How much did you make?"

She wiped her hand on her shirt. "I wasn't doing it for the money."

Her voice was a touch higher than I expected it to be.

I was going to try and put my hand in the snack bowl at the same time as hers to see if I could touch it and to see what she would do if I did. But right then the lights were turned up. We looked around to see Officer O'Connell and Aaron and Jake trying to herd people out of the cafeteria. Later I found out they cut the social short because of Jamie's dalliance with Nurse

Feingard. Which, of course, would happen the one time I was actually *talking* to someone.

We made eye contact for one second. She wiped her hand on her shirt again, looked around, and goes, "Well, see ya." I was like, "Yeah." For some reason I wanted to be the first one to turn around and walk away. So I practically shot over to where everyone from my suite was gathering with Aaron, which, in retrospect, seems a little unnecessary.

Another thing about her is that she's really tall.

What It's Like to Hit an Old Man in the Head with a Gun I

It's like anything else. You ever check out a library book? Or buy something at a store? Or jump off some steps into a lake? It's just something that happens in time and space; you do it and then it's done. Except in this specific instance, you happen to have a crumpled person at your feet getting smears of blood on the dusty linoleum floor. But it's not like you've changed. You're still you, in your same body. You can still spell. The basic society of your brain is still the same. You're breathing. People do things. Things happen all the time.

It was lukewarm in that store, not cold. And the light was flickering like it would have if it was a movie and this was something I was doing in a movie. A packet of pills fell out of a little cardboard display box and landed on the floor with a cellophane thud. They said "Last Longer!" I heard a car speed off outside and it didn't occur to me that it could be Craig's.

What It's Like to Hit an Old Man in the Head with a Gun II

Tiring. My legs felt as heavy as filing cabinets. Earlier that night, me and Craig had been sitting in the Jerry's Subs on Whittaker.

A girl from our high school was working behind the sandwich counter, pulling plastic wrap over all the buckets of lettuce and tomatoes. Other than us three it was empty. We had done all our coke and my throat stung and I couldn't figure out if I was still fucked up or not.

We weren't really talking because there was nothing to talk about. The gun was in the glove compartment of his van. It was Refrigerator Man's. It didn't take me long to find it in our house. It was in, of all places, one of the many empty cabinets in our kitchen—shoved toward the back among some sawdust and insect carcasses. All I had to do was pick it up.

We decided on the 7-Eleven on Karmen Street next to the old gutted-out Protestant church because it was fairly secluded. On one side were trees and on the other were some huge Dumpsters, and also because it was usually deserted, especially late at night. The guy who worked there was this old dude who was perpetually holding the remote control of the television midair with his mouth dangling open. So yeah, those were the things we knew. It's not like we were sitting around making pie charts about it, though.

I mean, you want to pull off some quotidian crime, like something obvious and boring and easy like ripping off a convenience store, and you think you know enough about what to do just from movies and stuff—you basically do I guess. But then you're getting handcuffed and you're like, "Do over!"

Like I said, the gun was in the glove compartment. It was a pretty warm night. We were out of coke and wandering around Braddock Town Center waiting for it to get late enough for us to drive over there. We went to the mega-bookstore and looked at magazines. We sat in this little gazebo and listened to the restaurant jazz that was being piped into the open air from somewhere. Craig was like, "I want some fries." I said, "Implied."

If you have a gun pointed at your head, it's usually an incentive to do what you're told. Not so for Derek Manager, as the little name tag on his shirt called him, who "managed" to just stare at me like I was a pair of fluffy shoes in his closet. When I came into the store, with all of the sweaty, teenage fury I could muster (I decided to go with unhinged and hair-trigger crazy rather than calm and calculating, which, obviously, was not the right tactic because I think it just ended up being confusing) and started screaming and pointing the gun and telling Derek Manager to open the cash register, he was in his usual stance, staring at the television with the remote control midair, and he did only a half turn in my direction to accommodate my arrival. So now I'm pointing the gun at him, at his stupid white-haired, blue-veined temple, and he's pointing the remote at me and I kind of just want to forget the whole thing.

But I don't. I yell something like, "Fucking *move it! Move it!* Fucking do it!" or some variety of the kind of thing you're supposed to say in that situation when he lowers his remote and goes all feebly, "D-d-d-don't h-h-hurt me." And that's when I jump over the counter and hit him, hard, in the head, with the side of my (unloaded, I might mention, although that didn't seem to matter to the judge) gun. It made a dull, wet sound that I didn't expect.

He deflates. Falls from the air. Crumples at my feet. And then it's quiet. And I'm so tired. The light is flickering. I see myself from the outside, standing there in this sagging 7-Eleven, just a poor mixed-up kid caught in a riptide of violence. Or no, I see myself as a sand dune, moved slightly one way in the wind, my gun connecting with Derek Manager's head in a moment of ancient synchronicity because it was always *going* to happen.

He's crowded around my feet and I feel like I'm in a quicksand of old man. I have to kick him in order to move around. There are smears of blood on the floor. A packet of pills falls out of its display box. I hear a car speed away. My legs feel as heavy as filing cabinets. I just didn't want to *be* there anymore. And then that kind of worked out because then the cops were there. No warning. No sirens from a distance getting closer and closer. A swarm of them just suddenly around me.

I wanted to tell them: I would do it again. I would do it again because it's true what they say about old people: they're just like babies and look at you all hollow and scared and you just want to bash their heads in and watch the pieces scatter into darkness.

Second Cousins

Lane. Can. Suck. It. Today is Friday, and that means only one thing: another helping of window pane, another stop on the silence campaign, another session with Lane. As usual, Officer O'Connell escorted me to her office at eleven o'clock. As usual, she was playing Solitaire on her computer and looked surprised to see me and then started massaging her temple as if I gave her a headache, and said, "Fine. Hello, Jacob. Please sit." As usual I slumped down onto the denim sofa and picked up and held the denim pillow.

What at once annoys and amuses me about Lane is her complete inability to conceal how much she dislikes me. I'm just like this freight of dead teenage weight that ladens her Friday afternoon each week and it's all she can do to marshal the appropriate energy to convince me that she *doesn't* think I'm a foregone conclusion. This is how we compose our faces: me in an expression so neutral I like to think it makes me almost invisible. Hers in a kind of set, bored expectancy. She makes a big deal out of shuffling the papers in my folder at the beginning of each session as if there's so much headway we've made that she has to go over before we can get to the next glimmering plane of analysis.

Anyway, the reason today's session sucked so much harder than usual was that Lane has taken it upon herself to introduce a crappy new element into my life. She obviously, in her finely tuned assessment, decided what I need is another incredibly awkward relationship with an adult. In other words, she wants me to meet with a sponsor.

She was like, "Jacob, have you heard of the sponsor program here?"

Silence.

"We've found that it's been quite successful with many of our young people."

Silence.

"I think you could benefit from a positive influence."

Silence.

"It's called 'Second Cousins.' And it's the flagship program out in Kingsbury County. It's been quite successful there." And now I see that she's got a folder that spells out "Second Cousins" on the front in rippling letters like a pond that someone dropped a pebble into.

Would you be willing to meet with someone?"

"No."

"Why not?"

"Because I don't fucking want to."

"Please do not swear at me."

Silence.

"For instance, Eddie Alvarez has expressed interest in becoming a veterinarian, and we were able to match him up with a sponsor who works at a pet store. Eddie will be leaving the center soon, and once he gets out, he may be able to work at the store and get some experience with animals."

Silence.

"In other words, there are many adults out there . . . *people* with jobs, families, lives, who are interested in being there for troubled young adults like yourself. They offer their time and are willing to be there for you, during your sentence, and once you've completed it, so that you have someone you can count on."

Silence. But at this point, I already know what's coming. I already know that despite her pretending to ask me my opinion, despite the fact that we're supposedly discussing it, she's already signed me up and there is some normal guy with like, magazine subscriptions and a clean car waiting behind the door ready to be a positive influence, completely unaware that our no doubt excruciatingly awkward interactions will only further embitter me toward humankind.

"I've signed you up for a meeting on Wednesday."

"Is it with some garlic bread?"

"No."

"Some bread sticks?"

"It's with a person. Named Jim. And I would urge you to give him a chance, or else in your evaluation it will become clear that you're not open to this kind of thing."

There you have it. Vintage Lane. My evaluation determines whether I can get out of here on time.

The S&P Index

Okay, but I'm not done writing about this, because I can't sleep and there is this anger in me right now, changing and morphing and pulling tides up and down through my chest and stomach.

So we're still sitting there, me in resigned silence, her in administrative triumph (I saw her actually exaggeratedly "check" something off in my folder after our "talk" about my sponsor), when she asks me some questions about what I'm planning to do once I leave here, to which I'm even more unresponsive than usual, and she kind of slams her pen and folder in her lap and goes, "Okay, listen," in this voice that let me know I was in for a variety of hard truths (every once in a while Lane gets into a hard-truth mode), and as usual I was right.

She starts going off about life after the center. And what was I going to do. That we all have problems but at some point you have to get over them and move on. And that at some point I was going to have to figure out how to make a life for myself. And figure out how to function in the world. And go out there and heat up food in a microwave and buy a car and think about Niagara Falls and do all the rest of the stuff that everyone else does all the time. I mean, that's not exactly what she said but it's what she *meant*.

I did what I never do, which was to convey some emotion, which manifested itself in my shifting on the sofa and tightening my grip on the denim pillow. I was getting really pissed off at Lane talking to me like she was blowing my mind. Like I'm an idiot.

It's not like I don't know *how* to be a person who functions outside of here. I'm pretty well schooled in the deadened adult compromise it takes to secure some valid state of being in the world. But I don't fucking care, because I know something already that most people learn only once they've reached the end of whatever personal disappointment corridor they've started on, a secret shoved way down deep into the butt pocket of the universe, which is that everything, no matter what, is totally sad and completely pointless.

For instance, possibly the saddest thing that exists, is an insect zoo.

A couple of years ago, during one of my mom and Refrigerator Man's short-lived periods of sobriety, Beans went ahead and decided what we needed was a forced family outing. Being so close to our nation's capital, she thought we could take advantage of the many museums and suggested we go to the Insect Zoo at the Museum of Natural History, which she saw featured on public access television in between the sassy judge shows she so adores in the afternoons.

She suggested it one summer night when, by some rare circumstance, like the stars aligning a certain way every thousand years, we were all in the kitchen at the same time. Her face beamed with pathetic gratitude when Refrigerator Man said distractedly, "Fine, whatever. You have to drive, though," as a cloud of sawdust whirled around his head from the holes he was inexplicably drilling in our cabinets. Then she looked at me and goes, "Insect Zoo? Hon? Huh?"

So the following Saturday we all pile into her Ford Escort with the screwy axle and head downtown. Refrigerator Man is wearing a clean shirt and seems vaguely embarrassed as he gets into the car. By mile two he's drinking from his flask. Before we get on the beltway he makes Beans pull over at a gas station so he can buy beer. She says something under her breath. He says, "C'mon, Erin-o, you've gotta let a man calm his nerves from your driving." He ruffles her hair. She hitches up a smile.

The ride is quiet except for Beans messing with the radio dial until Refrigerator Man swats her hand away and turns the dial to a classic rock station. Some song comes on and he goes, "Yeah, tell it to Kelly," in reference to who knows what. And that's when I look at him looking out the window and get a faint whiff of the garbage dump of experiences he's sitting on and wonder, not for the first time, who he is and where he came from and how he beached himself on our lives.

It's sunny out and Refrigerator Man, still in the wake of the song, opens the window and puts his hand out, kid-style, to feel the wind. After a second he seems embarrassed again, shuts the window, kind of recomposes his body, and looks around. It's like he's trying to tune into the correct frequency of how to be. He gets frustrated and pulls on the flask.

I'm sitting in the backseat watching all of this happen because I've become somewhat of an expert on the different stages of his inebriation all the way up until the end, when he turns into driftwood.

Exhibit A: With the first flush of alcohol, he will seem refreshed and resort to a kind of jocular behavior that many women in his past, including my mom, have probably found charming. In this case, he draws a pair of tits in the dust on the dashboard, points to them and goes, "What?" Cue the raspy, smoke-logged laughter of desperate adults.

It's a big, bright, sunny day, like a canvas for good-natured outings. Beans is wearing a huge red belt I've never seen before. If she notices how drunk Refrigerator Man is, she's not saying anything. She has the air of someone whose mission it is to carry a huge boulder across a shoulder-deep lake. And she looks at the Museum of Natural History, which is austere and cold-seeming, like a long vocabulary word you don't know the meaning of, with an expression of determination I'm not used to. I know what she's thinking: that maybe we should have dressed up a little. We climb the steps and walk into the museum tentatively, like you would onto a swaying barge.

We've bought tickets (with a wad of money Beans withdrew from her purse, upsetting a nest of lip gloss tubes in the process, one of which fell out and rolled across the floor to where it stopped at a museum guard's foot, at which point we all exchanged weird glances), and now we're in some kind of echo-y atrium with a rearing elephant in the middle. My mom has somehow already managed to accrue a large number of pamphlets. She's holding them to her chest and looking around helplessly. I see a sign leading to a musty-looking hallway that says "Insect Zoo."

Exhibit B: Refrigerator Man will start to walk like his shoelaces are tied together. The top of his body will lurch forward while his feet do a hemmed-in shuffle to catch up. We follow the sign, my mom leading the way while nervously stuffing pamphlets into her bag, then me, and Refrigerator Man stumbling along behind us.

In the middle of the Insect Zoo is a slightly foggy hexagonal Plexiglas case covering a sort of castle of honeycomb with a blanket of surging bees on it. I stand there looking at it. A school group jostles past me. The air is moist and close. There is a guard at the entrance rocking back and forth on his feet, and I don't know if I'm being paranoid or if he really has been watching me this whole time.

I wish I could touch the honeycomb. At certain places the bodies of the bees seem to be lined up. I wonder why everything they make is hexagonal. I wonder if they think in hexagons. I wonder if they make things in hexagons because the hexagon is the actual shape of the universe. I'm thinking of all this, actually having a wonder-of-nature moment when I hear a familiar voice behind me say, "Badass spiders!" a little too loudly. I turn around. Refrigerator Man's shirt is half untucked and his eyes are aquariums.

Exhibit C: When he's really drunk, Refrigerator Man will act like he's the dapper star of a one-person comedy revue. Oblivious to everything around him, he'll beam, his face shining as if he's turning to a stadium of booming applause. He'll think that everything he does is pure comic gold and he's encased and alone in a spotlight of approval. So when, despite the look of frozen terror on Erin's face, he takes her hand and forces it against the Plexiglas hexagon and yells, "Afraid of bees! Afraid of bees!" and she tries to yank herself away with a force that ends up spraining her wrist, he doesn't notice the widening spill of silence around us, or the harried, embarrassed expressions of other adults. He's grandstanding, riffing, participating in a hilarious slapstick number to tides of imagined laughter. And Erin, my mom, is flailing around like an upended beetle.

Seeing her look like that? Not when she was scared but when she had gotten up, straightened herself out, and saw the guard coming and looked around and kind of assessed everything and her whole face fell? No kidding. I would rather watch a space station explode in midair.

My mom's face, in that moment, was a variegated tapestry of disappointment. She looked around in this way where you could tell everything was crystallizing in front of her—the whole stupid landscape of the day and everything that had led up to it. Our eyes locked and hers were apologetic. But there was something else, too. I saw her relegate me to the rest of it. I was something else that hadn't worked out.

So yeah. Going to an Insect Zoo, among other things, is very, very sad and pointless and so is everything else and everyone can bow down and suck it at the altar of that one specific truth.

Jesus Christ and Empty Afternoons

In complete disregard for whatever section of the Constitution mandates that there should be a separation of Church and State, the JDC is doing everything it can to convert itself into a Christian training camp. Among the initiatives are the Bible study classes, which we're not required, but heavily encouraged, to attend, as well as the moment of silence we now take before each meal where I'm like, "Great. Thanks for this Sloppy Joe. I want to kill myself."

At the center of this campaign is a sneakers-wearing self-proclaimed "code-red procrastinator" who also goes by the name of Pastor Todd, and who has his very own office here, right next to the rec room. When Pastor Todd is not apprising me of the fact that "Jesus was so badass he once knocked over a table," or attempting to high-five me in the hallway, he is trying to get me to come to the Bible study classes, which, I would rather eat a mug of ice cream with a bunch of hair in it.

I've had my own experiences with religion, namely the time I went with Rocky to a youth group meeting in our middle school's auditorium where everyone walked around like mini-parents and the highly advertised pizza was definitely in short supply.

Also, my mom once dated this Christian soccer-coach man-child named Dale who actually wasn't that bad except that he was one of those people you can't really talk to because he always had a prepared answer for everything.

So anyway, I was sitting in my room for free time the other day, writing in this very notebook, when none other than Pastor Todd just happens to "drop by." He knocks on my door (which was open because it's required to be) like he just happened to be there and decided to say hello as an afterthought. Which I know isn't the way it really went down in his head, because I can tell that Pastor Todd has been watching me ever since I got here because I'm one of the only ones who don't go to his Bible study classes.

This was further evidenced later when we were in his office and he goes, "I've been watching you, Jake." (But only after sitting on the corner of his desk in a manner that I'm pretty sure was supposed to be perceived as impromptu, and staring at me in this "let's cut to the chase" way. The only reason I went to his office is because I, too, want to cut to the chase because I'm really ready for him to leave me alone.)

Another thing about Pastor Todd is he has that kind of caustic cheerfulness that can only mask a dormant hostility. Sometimes he'll say something a certain way and you'll kind of want to shield your face. For instance, when we first sat down, apropos of nothing, he looks up and clenches his fists and goes, "Life!" really loudly and then had to sort of recompose himself.

There was a green plastic model of a building on his desk. It resembled an alien Eiffel Tower, and on the bottom, on the stand, it said "The Space Needle." I accidentally looked at it and our eyes met a few times and I could tell he was warming up to say something. I stared at my lap, and, thankfully, he retreated. It was quiet for a few moments. He shifted in his chair.

Finally he says, "It's so funny. Me and you. Sitting here." He goes, "Two people who would never have met if it wasn't for these"—and then he looks around the room and kind of chuckles to himself—"circumstances." Then he gets all enthusiastic again, looks up, and goes, "Oh, man!" He picks up a paperweight, puts it down. "I meet so many kids, just like you, who think that everyone has forgotten about them. They think it's over, that no one cares. And I get to tell them that that's not *true*."

Then he gets up from the edge of the desk, walks around it, sits down across from me, and proceeds to take things down a notch. He's like, "Jake, I just want to ask you a question. Do you feel as if you have a purpose in life?"

Now I'm feeling really uncomfortable, as I always do when sitting point-blank across from an adult who is trying to pry me open with softball questions that are meant to lead to a discussion the outcome of which they've already decided. So I just sit there, staring off into the distance, blank as a cow in a field.

Pastor Todd goes, "Look, I've seen your file, I can tell that you're gifted." And then he seems to change his mind and he shifts in his chair and makes a little steeple with his hands and says, "Let me tell you a story."

He sits back. "This is a story about a man, a boy, someone just like you or me...or no. This is a story about a kid in trouble." And that's when I realize what has always bugged me the most about Pastor Todd, besides his lamely constructed persona: it's that you get the sense that he's always trying to make everything into an epic movie. Like everyone is writhing in some cinematic rinse cycle of redemption.

He's like, "Okay, this is a story about me, when I was a very angry young man. A story about a father and son. I used to live in West Virginia with my family. My father owned a landscaping business, and let's just say that we did not get along." Then Pastor Todd leans back and laughs and goes, "We *hated* each other. Oh yes, we did. I was deeply, deeply unhappy. I lived in the basement and I was addicted to"—and this is where I perked up and actually started listening for a second, until he said—"caffeine. Caffeine and computer games. Myst, Castle Wolfenstein, you name it, I played it all night long. I was a shut-in. Completely miserable. In the den. Playing by myself with all the lights off. Night after night. I was searching for something."

At this point Pastor Todd reached down below his desk and pulled out a bottle of water, unscrewed the cap with an overly violent twist of his hand and took a swig.

"I was in a chapel of my own alienation," he said, exhaling. "My god was a revolving variety of guns. My mission was always to get to the next 'level.' Not a good scene. But then something happened. One afternoon, everything changed."

He smiled to himself and looked into the distance.

"Sometimes, during the summer, I would help my father with his landscaping business. He did work for some wealthy people up around McLean. Like I said before, we were not on very good terms. One afternoon, after a fight, he sent me to the hardware store to buy some mulch. It was a hot day. The sun was pounding down and I had to carry all these bags across the parking lot. I remember feeling burdened. Burdened by the mulch and burdened by anger. I was having violent thoughts about my father. I felt everything crashing inward. And then"—Pastor Todd opened his hands like two separate sunbursts and held them in the air—"it came to me. A voice. Clear as a cool stream through a field. It said, 'Go to your father, put your hand on his shoulder, tell him that you love him.'"

Then Pastor Todd sat back and started talking in a more businesslike way.

"Now, I'd always heard about "God" and "Jesus Christ" and all of that stuff, but I'd never thought it was for me. But somehow I knew, that day, that our Lord was speaking to me in that parking lot. And that I should do what he said. So, indeed, I went home to my father. I put my hand on his shoulder. I said, 'I love you, Father,' and it was…awkward. But it was also a turning point. Things got better for me after that."

I stared at a cardboard crate of mini bottled waters in the corner of the room. There was a little vista of pine trees on each label.

Finally Pastor Todd was like, "Jake, do you understand what I'm saying? That was God talking to me in the parking lot. Telling me to not only love my father but to love Him. Because He is *our* Father."

In my head I was like, "Yeah, Pastor Todd. I get what you're saying. But I don't understand why your fucked-up magic story is supposed to have any bearing on me. Since when does hearing a supernatural being talking to you in a parking lot and then doing its bidding not make you insane? And since when does that give you the authority to sit here and try to convert me to some religion where you can't have sex?" But I didn't say any of that. I just sat there.

Pastor Todd was like, "This has been fun, and I think we've made some... dare I say it? Progress?"

I shifted in my seat.

He goes, "How 'bout we have another one of our rap sessions sometime next week?"

I was like, "That's not—" But then he interrupted me and goes, "Great! Looking forward to it."

And then we silently walked back to my room.

Fake Wooden Desks

Okay. When I first got here I thought, for some reason, that I wouldn't have to go to school, or take classes. That turned out to be the exact opposite of the truth. Every day we have to go to classroom 107A, where portions of English, math, and social studies are meted out like the different nutrients of a hospital diet. Classroom 107A seems to be positioned right on top of the bored/tired divide in the sterile tundra of this building. Every day is like a half-cognizant wade through swamps of stupid information, and then I sometimes get busted for not paying attention, and I'm like, "Listen, Hassle (Roy Hassle. Our teacher. Thrice-divorced alcoholic), I could tabulate and process and analyze everything you just told me and make it bendy with understanding within like, five minutes of actual thought if I wanted to, so don't pretend like I'm going *miss* something if I don't hang on to everything you say." Of course, I don't say that because if I did it would get back to Lane and thus would begin a whole backward bureaucratic process that would prevent me from getting out of this Rubik's Cube of misguided intentions on time.

Classroom 107A sits across from two bathrooms in the middle of a nondescript hallway. The chairs, which are stuck to the floor along with the desks, are made with some bullshit plastic polymer material that's really slick, so it's impossible to fall asleep, because you can literally slide to the ground like a heap of sheets. So every once in a while, you'll hear someone have a miniseizure in their chair as they jolt awake and straighten themselves out midglide. Other than that, it's pretty much the blandest room on the most remote outer banks of blandness. There is a big desk at the front for the teacher. And a clunky overhead projector relegated to the corner like a lesser-known dinosaur skeleton.

Usually I just sit and somehow the time passes, and I'd even gotten into a rhythm where I didn't notice I was there. But today all of that changed. We got a new teacher. Hassle has been replaced by a short, clipboard-holding, vest-wearing, no-breast-having, jumping cable of a woman named Janet Stipling, and so far she has proved to be a car-size thorn in my ass.

If there was one message I could write in the sky with clouds, it would be that just because you survived a double mastectomy doesn't mean you can scream at people at eight-thirty in the morning.

I was just putting the finishing touches on a shark mural I'd drawn on my desk, figuring it would probably be another twenty minutes before Hassle finally shuffled in, when right on time, we heard someone clear their throat and looked up to see a woman holding the aforementioned clipboard and looking at us like she was all pissed.

She goes, in a wiry southern accent, "My *name* is Janet Stipling. I am going to *replace* Mr. Hassle."

She heaves a huge, dusty quilted bag onto the desk.

She starts slowly walking down the classroom and looking at everyone, wearing a boxy vest that has actual seashells and coins sewn onto it. As she came my way, I gave her my pretty standard-issue, lazy-eyed, smirking-up-and-down, "I'm-going-to-rape-you-and-you'll-secretly-like-it" look that messes up most women, especially middle-aged ones for at least a few seconds. But she shot a death stare in my direction so harsh it might have actually sterilized me.

She gets back to the front of the room and goes, or more like shouts (because apparently she has to shout everything. It's like she's got a little cannon in her mouth that blasts out sentence after knuckly sentence), "All right! Now I told you my name and I will tell you something else, case you think you can mess with me, because you can't. A while ago" — and then she pointed to her chest — "I lost both of *these*."

She thumped her chest with her fist and all the seashells and coins sewn onto her vest rattled.

"Flat as a buzz cut under this cotton material." Then she goes, "Do you think I survived a double mastectomy and a trial separation all in the same year just so I could come here and be messed with by a bunch of kids? Well, do you?" We all just sat there. "Because I did not." Then she stepped back and looked around the room. "Long as we got that straight, we shouldn't have any problems."

She walks to the front of the room and starts looking through her large bag. She rummages around and withdraws, not without some difficulty, a shiny, new, floppy workbook similar to the ones we were issued when we came here. Except this one has a picture of a smiling Hispanic kid getting onto a bus. She holds it up. It says *Passports, 7.0* on it.

"Now," she says, "how far have you gotten in this?"

We are as quiet and still as elk.

"Hello?" she says, looking around. "All right, fine." She puts the book down and looks at her clipboard, running her finger up and down what I'm assuming was a list of our names. And call me psychic but I knew, more than I've ever known anything else in my life, where her finger was going to stop. "Mr. Jacob Higgins."

"Yeah?" I'm sitting in the corner, and she snaps her head toward me as if she were in the pitch dark and just heard something coming from my direction.

"Where are you in this workbook?" She's picked it up again and is holding it in the air for me to see.

"I don't...know."

"Do you *have* this workbook?"

"I don't know."

"Did you *lose* this workbook?"

"No?"

"*Passports,*" she says, turning away from me and showing the book to the rest of the class. "*Passports!*" she yells. She looks back at her clipboard. "Mr. Perkins!" Jamie Perkins winces. "Where are you in this workbook?"

He sits up and withdraws a dusty workbook from his desk. It has a girl wearing a huge sweater on the cover. It says *Passports, 6.9.*

"That's the workbook you were issued when you came here?" He nods.

"When did you come here?"

Jamie goes, "Uh."

"And I've got this one," says Desean Phillips from the back of the room. He's holding up a workbook with two people on the cover sitting on a park bench and smiling at each other as they hold up their newspapers in an improvised madcap moment. It says *Passports, 6.0* on it.

"Well, what in the..." Janet Stipling looks at her workbook and then around the room. "Does *anyone* have this workbook?" She holds it up again.

Two people raise their hands.

"That's just perfect," she says. "That's just great." She flips through the workbook. "All right, let me ask you this. What was the last thing you *covered* in this class? Doesn't matter what workbook you have."

No one says anything.

"A topic," she says. "What was the last thing you talked about?"

Someone coughs.

Stipling slams the book shut. "*Hello*, am I going to have to—"

"The cotton gin," says Eddie Alvarez.

"The cotton gin?"

"Yeah, Hassle said something about the cotton gin."

"A bald eagle," says Desean Phillips.

Stipling squints her eyes. "Excuse me, Mr. . . ."

"Desean."

"Phillips, Desean Phillips," she says, looking at her clipboard.

"Yeah, there was a bald eagle."

Stipling looks up at him and then around the room. "Wonderful," she says. "Fine."

She scribbles something on her clipboard and then slams it on the desk, then picks it up again and jots something down in the corner. She starts going through her bag, pricks herself on something inside, snatches her hand out and starts studying her thumb with concentrated anger. She finally takes out the exact same kind of blue binder that Hassle had and starts checking things off.

"Now listen *up!*" she says, looking at us. "Whatever workbook you were given when you got here, you will bring to class tomorrow. I don't care what edition you have, just find it and bring it. Any questions?"

She started walking up and down the aisles and saying that once we got the workbooks sorted out, we were going to start turning in homework. Then she told us to stop looking at her like dumb cattle, because that's her number one pet peeve. ("You all know what a *pet peeve* is? It is a low-grade irritation.") Then she told us to get out a piece of paper and write down everything we knew about the Civil War, because apparently that's the unit we were supposed to be working on. And then she gave us yet another assignment, which was to think of a topic to write a paper on.

So yeah. But I know all about teachers that get in your face like that. Behind their hostile exterior they're all panhandlers for potential. They come from the same tough-love-scared-straight school of teaching where they think we're all sooty angels deep down inside and with a little bit of American renegade teaching magic we'll start turning in math problems on clean, unwrinkled pieces of paper and start following elections or some shit.

But here's the problem with teachers like Stipling: even though you can see the levers and pulleys in their personality, say you decide, for whatever reason, to dispense actual interest in something they're teaching, or ask a question that indicates you've been listening. What happens is they try not to fumble the moment even as they're welling up with all sorts of good intentions and the feeling that they've been able to *crack* you. The problem now is they're going to have expectations, and so you become saddled with the glances and overtures of said teacher. But you know it's not going to lead anywhere and so you feel kind of bad for them and wish you'd never said anything in the first place.

How do you diffuse a situation like that? You do something that completely recalibrates the way they think about you. Like, for instance, you draw a messed-up picture of a stick figure dismembering other stick figures that have uncannily similar physical characteristics to said teacher's colleagues and you leave it around for them to find. And then they realize they're not dealing with some poor underserved kid with a heart of gold, but rather with a suburban psychopath. And nobody wants to fuck with that.

Andrea Episode in Which She Tells Me Weird Shit About Her Past

Every day the JDC takes it upon itself to circulate us through actual outside air for half an hour in order to convince us that our sentences here are not cruel and unusual. At exactly four-thirty each afternoon, weather permitting, we're shoved out into the courtyard and invited to sit on one of the four steel benches, play basketball on the cracked concrete, or lean against a wall.

On nice days, when the sky is blue, the sense of relief I get from feeling the sun on my face is always chased by the realization that I'm going to have to go inside soon, and that is when my stomach attempts to have an insurgency. So usually I'll just sit on one of the red steel benches and look down and do this meditation thing where I try as hard as I can to block out all sense perception and turn into pure organic material that doesn't have to consider anything or do anything ever.

Another thing about the courtyard is that the alchemy of certain people out there affects the levels of palpable hostility and likelihood of fights breaking out, so they do this rotation thing where there are different batches of inmates together at different times.

So today Andrea was there. When I noticed her standing against the wall looking into the distance like she was trying to remember something, my self-imposed blackout dissolved and I became interested in my surroundings. Through one of the windows I saw Lane walk down the hallway. There was a bird chirping. Jamie Perkins was motioning to this guy Bryan over by the water fountain like he was trying to convince him of something. Then I looked back to Andrea.

Since the social, my thoughts about her have run the gamut from "When are we going to do it?" to "I wonder if God's plan involves me ever getting to finger Andrea." I pretended that I didn't see her at first and focused my attention on a deflated basketball sitting in the shade. When I looked again, we made eye contact. And then a second later she was walking toward me. She came up to me and was like, "Hey man," and made a plank with her hands to shield her eyes from the sun.

I was like, "What's up?"

She goes, "Um, nothing."

Eddie came up and threw a basketball at me and was like, "Play?" And I threw it back at him and was like, "Nah."

At this point Andrea was sitting next to me and looking down at her hand and pushing the skin around on it.

She goes, "Can you like, *mail letters* here? I need to mail a letter."

"Like a real letter?"

"Yeah."

I didn't have the answer to this question. But I decided to say something semi-official sounding, which, I don't even know why I would give a crap about impressing Andrea via my knowledge of the appropriate channels of correspondence at the JDC. I should have just waited for the opportunity to say something funny.

But I said, "Um. Yeah...you probably have to take it to the main office or something. Give it to Jan. Or like, ask your suite counselor."

We sat in silence for a while and then I was like, "Where's the letter going?"

She was like, "You mean like, where do I want to send it?"

"Yeah."

"Alaska. It's where my older brother lives.

"Oh. Is he a...canner?"

"Huh?"

"Canner? A fish canner? Like at a cannery?"

"No. He's a glassblower. He makes bongs and sells them on the Internet."

"Oh."

"And sometimes pumpkin vases, for Thanksgiving."

"Okay."

"And sometimes Easter eggs."

"Fair enough."

And then I don't remember exactly what was said next but we ended up talking about her messed-up sister.

She was like, "Me and Cassie were really close up until I turned twelve and she turned fourteen. I got really into Stonehenge. You know? In England? And she suddenly started thinking that she was ugly. She wanted a nose job. It's all she ever talked about."

"That's weird."

"I know. She thought she was really ugly."

Every now and then I would dart my eyes up to Andrea's face. She was blushing. And there were faint continents of redness on her neck.

"Was she?"

"No. I mean, I don't know. Our stepmom said she looked 'earthy.'

"It was all she ever talked about," Andrea continued. She pinched up her face.

"Nose job, nose job, nose job. Our dad told her that she should get a real job. That made her really mad. A few times I walked in on her in the bathroom in front of the mirror, just staring at herself. I never knew how long she'd been standing there."

Andrea pushed some hair behind her ear. She has lots of new baby hairs along her hairline.

She looked at me and sat up straight. "Do you have any siblings?" She seemed uncomfortable by the way she'd said *siblings*, so then she said, "brothers or sisters?"

"Nah," I said. "No."

"One time my sister took a microwave dinner and cleaned it out so it was just the plastic tray, with the compartments? She stomped it on the floor and yelled that she was going to cut her nose off herself."

"That's fucked up."

"So that night, I lay in my bed in my room and stared at the ceiling. . . . You know how sometimes they're painted so you can see the brushstrokes?"

I nodded.

"I stared at the brushstrokes. I was so high."

Across the courtyard, Jamie Perkins picked up the caved-in basketball, wiped a palm on his pants, and let the ball thud to the ground. I watched Aaron check his watch and look around.

"So what happened?" I said. I didn't want her to stop talking. The more she spoke, the more I could sense these touchstones in the way she formed her words, like eventually I would be able to follow them down a path to the center of her being.

"You mean with my sister?"

"Yeah." I pushed my thumb into an embedded nail on the bench and then stared at the imprint it made on my skin.

"Well," Andrea sighed, "she was getting really messed up about it. Crying and stuff and saying she wouldn't go to school.

My stepmom and dad didn't know what to do. They would try to get her out of bed and she would be like liquid, they could get handfuls, but they couldn't get her up all at once. She would yell, 'It's just a medical *procedure!*' I mean, what are you supposed to do when you know someone who thinks they're that ugly?"

We made eye contact for one second.

"What are you supposed to tell someone who wakes up every day thinking that they got the wrong face? That their nose and eyes and mouth aren't organized?"

I breathed in to say something, but then Andrea kept talking.

"It like, ate her up. It even got to my stepmom, who is usually a total werewolf bitch. She said to my sister, 'Listen, honey,' all nice and soft, but it didn't help. Cassie just got worse. She was like a big bruise walking around all the time. So finally, my dad took out a second mortgage or something like that and paid for her to get a nose job."

Andrea looked off into the distance.

"And?" I said.

"I mean..." She started pushing the skin around on her hand again. "Nothing ever really works out, you know?"

She started talking more forcefully and I noticed that she was bending her fingers back, one by one.

"I don't know why anyone thinks anything will ever work out. It doesn't. Someone'll smile at me and I'll be like, 'Yeah right, that's not going to work out.'"

I wasn't sure what to say. I was starting to feel a little uncomfortable. I squinted up at the sky. Sitting there with Andrea, with her talking so quickly, felt a little embarrassing. It was like she was the underside of a leaf, smarting and naked and veiny.

She held her hand midair, twisted it like she was using a doorknob.

"When she came back and they took all the bandages off and everything," she said, "looking at my sister's face was like walking down a different hallway to get to the same linen closet." Her hands fell into her lap.

"Is she okay?" I said.

"I don't know," said Andrea. "She still stands in the bathroom and looks at herself forever. I mean I haven't seen her for a few weeks. But I bet that's what she's doing right now."

We sat quietly for a while. I kicked my sneakers together like to get dirt off them, even though there wasn't any.

"My therapist, David? He's always like, 'Why do you smoke so much weed?' and I'm like, 'I dunno.' I mean, *Jesus*."

"I know," I said.

I was going to start telling her about Lane, but then I looked around and noticed that we were the only ones still out there. There was a basketball rolling across the concrete and Aaron was walking toward us. He goes, "What's wrong with you two? Didn't you hear me calling you? It's time to go inside." We were both like, *"Okay."*

So then she went with the girls and I went with the guys and it was off to another mind-numbing half hour in the computer room for me. And then to the cafeteria where I picked at a pale block of something that defied classification, though I did hear the term *lasagna* being thrown around.

The thing is, when we were sitting out there on the bench, it was like I almost found a way out of being attracted to her and it was kind of a relief. Like there was something so bald about the way she was talking. But after we left the courtyard, I couldn't stop thinking about our conversation and the red continents on her neck. It was like we were in an invisible dome together, with our breath mingling in the airspace of our new property. And the way she would look up and blink and then look down all soft and then *softly* look back up; and the way when she was talking her face would melt and then harden with each new hinge in conversation, and how her words are webbed with a southern accent. And it's like I can't stop thinking about these specific things, even now, even as I write this during free time and the lights are about to go off—I can feel it. I can feel the subtle inhalation before the thudding half-light. And I'm noticing that but I'm also thinking about Andrea because it's like my brain is *stained* with her.

Coup d'Snack

A new kind of cookie has been added to the snack rotation. Apparently the pellet cookies have been phased out and replaced by a different interpretation on a theme, the theme being "how to employ this waxy type of chocolate that doesn't taste like anything." The new cookies are oval with divots in them, the whole thing half dipped in the aforementioned substance. At first I was like, "Maybe this'll be good." But I was quickly punished for my soaring optimism as soon as I put one in my mouth and realized that it tasted like concrete powder. It's the kind of thing that would only taste good if you were an astronaut who had lost touch with the home base and you had run out of things to eat until you like, *found* one of these.

So anyway. I ate one and then I was going to sit on my usual place on the sofa, but David Keffler was sitting there, so I sat on the floor next to the rack of STD pamphlets. Then when I leaned back on my hands, a staple that had been embedded in the carpet went up my fingernail and it totally hurt. I did not see Andrea today. And that pretty much sums it up for now.

David Encounter

Okay. I've known that David Keffler has wanted to talk to me the way you can tell that a car wants to cut in front of you a while before it does it. He traffics in knowing glances. He's always studying me for reactions to shit that happens in class and other places to see whether we have a common foundation of hatred on which we can build a friendship. I've learned to recognize this kind of thing because for some reason people always think I'm the one person who's going to collude with them, when really I pretty much always just want to be left alone.

Today in the rec room during snack time I was sitting on the sofa in my usual strawberry-wafer-induced sugar coma, staring at the whiteboard with the half-wiped-out piece of pie, trying not to think about anything, and not really bothering anyone. I was freezing, as usual; pitted by it, like the room was almost *sarcastically* cold.

I could feel David Keffler staring at me. He was over by the bookshelf, leaning against it in a fake-casual stance. I had a feeling he was going to try and talk to me and then suddenly he was there, holding out a soggy-looking strawberry wafer in his hand. He goes, "Want this?"

I struggled momentarily with the implications of what seemed to be an olive branch–type gesture and what might be invited if I took the wafer. I looked up at David. His face is strangely dented inward, and I got the usual chill of clinical evil I get whenever we make eye contact. But then I was like, "I guess." And took it from him and ate it.

He obviously thought this made us brothers of the half moon or something because he then sat down next to me on the couch. I tried to ward off any conversational advances by looking in the other direction and hunching over but he was like, "You have

Lane Davidson for therapy, right?" I was like, "Yeah," and continued looking away. Anyone even lightly schooled in body language would have understood that I was trying not to talk to anyone, but Keffler is apparently not too receptive to social cues.

He goes, "Yeah, me, too. Every Tuesday. I hate that cunt." And then he quickly looked at me and looked away.

I was like, "Yeah," and for the first time since I got here wanted snack time to be over.

"You know she's leaving soon, right?"

"No." Then I was mildly interested for like, two seconds, because I had always pictured Lane withering away in her denim office and playing Solitaire until the end of time.

"Yeah, she's married to this black guy and they're going to be missionaries in Africa."

I go, "Oh," and decide to go ahead and put that at the top of my list of facts that I will never think about again.

He threw a piece of cookie up in the air and then tilted his head back to catch it with his mouth in a gesture that in my calculation betrayed a sudden and misplaced arrogance. He went on.

"Yeah, my dad told me. He knows shit on all these people."

I started picking at a scab of dried gum on the arm of the sofa.

"You ever notice how all of her office is decorated in denim?"

I didn't say anything.

"I mean, what the fuck?"

I stretched my arms and legs out and yawned.

"She reminds me of my English teacher at Foxington. *Josephine.*"

Silence.

"She would always say it like that. *Josephine.* Like she was so sexy. And then she would stick her chest out."

He laughed quickly and in that way that people laugh when they're expecting you to laugh with them. But I didn't laugh. Number one, because it wasn't funny. Number two, because his comparison was way off. You can say a lot about Lane but one thing she doesn't try to project is sensuality.

"Don't you hate that?"

"Hate what?"

"Like when women..."

He trailed off and turned his head to the side. I really didn't want to be in that room anymore. It felt like an accident for me to be sitting there with David on that couch. I stared at the poster of the man wearing a soda-can suit. There was a blurry city street in the background.

David seemed to click back into a daydream. He goes, "She wore a gold watch. She'd always say, 'There's a story behind this watch.'"

Then he said, in a girly British accent, *"'My father was in the French foreign legion, and there's a real story behind this gold watch.'"*

He started heaving back and forth. I looked at him. His face was boiling with laughter and red.

"Do you know what I would do," he said, suddenly serious, "if I could get my hands on that watch? Do you know where I would put it?"

I felt pinned down by his gaze. I didn't answer.

"I would place it somewhere dark. And really, really tiny."

It suddenly felt warm in there. I pulled my shirt away from my chest and looked around. There was some activity in the corner by the snack bar where Jamie Perkins was pretending to have sex with one of the yellow octagonal chairs. Aaron was walking toward them.

I scanned the room for other people to talk to and was about to go over to Eddie and Desean, who were by the whiteboard, when David said, "She was there when I did it. It was in her class."

You usually find out why a person is here after a few days, and that then secures them a certain plot of reputation. But I haven't heard anything about David. As far as I know, no one knows what he did.

"What?" I said.

"She was there." He threw another piece of cookie into the air and tilted his head back to catch it. This time it hit him on the cheek and bounced down onto the sofa, which seemed to make him angry.

"Her mouth made a round O." He picked up his hand and drew an O in the air with his pointer finger. He started laughing again, soundlessly.

I looked around and wished there were more clocks in this building so that you weren't in a constant, dread-filled incubation of not knowing what time it was. I really wanted to get out of there.

"Logan," said David. "Logan Shiflett. I wonder what he's doing right now. I wonder if they let him keep his hand." He looked at me. "Do you think things should generally go faster? Or more slow?"

I didn't have a chance to answer.

"Armed robbery, right?" he said. "That's what you're here for?"

"I guess," I said, getting up.

"Nice. You whack anyone?"

I pretended like I didn't hear, stretched, and went over to Eddie and Desean. They were drawing their names on the whiteboard. I looked back at David briefly and he was staring into the distance with a little smirk. Snack time was over in like, two seconds anyway.

Second Cousins Meeting

There are parts of northern Virginia that are like, totally biodome, genetically engineered noon-day little squares with healthy cyborg people walking around like some pamphlet picture for a slightly fascist earth. It's all perfectly crafted grassy medians in the middle of freshly painted highways, drive-thrus, and tinted-glass buildings; people squinting as they unwrap their lunches on the benches outside in the little plaza of their office parks. There's nowhere to walk in the land of northern Virginia, no sidewalks or bike trails, only streets. So you'll see these office workers awkwardly loping up the grassy embankment of a highway to get to the Taco Bell on the other side during their lunch hour. The land of northern Virginia is antiseptic, air-conditioned, crafted, and full of disposable town centers.

The people who populate these centers, the droves of workers who fill up the buildings, all live in town houses next to the mall or the Metro. They're all thirty-five and use the same products and have really intense cell phones.

I happened to meet one of these people, adult variation number 432 of thirty-something male of the northern Virginia series, today in the cafeteria as part of the Second Cousins program that Lane is forcing me to participate in. I had forgotten about this particular blight on my life until I found myself being led by Aaron, along with Denise and Jamie, to the cafeteria during what was supposed to be courtyard time.

There were three people sitting there, three regulars on the responsibility circuit come to show us how to drink expensive water and fold up huge maps and make elaborate salads or whatever it is that normal people do all the time. One was a woman in a business suit who had a swirly hairdo and looked like she probably smelled really good. One was a guy wearing a shark's-tooth necklace and a leather jacket with tassels coming off the elbows. And one was the guy who I realized, as Jamie and Denise kept walking, was my "second cousin." He was hunched over and deftly thumbing a message into a shiny black miniature communication device.

This is such bullshit that I even have to do this. I generally do not like talking to people. I especially do not like talking to people at an enforced meeting in a cold cafeteria. I really especially do not like talking to people when the idea is that they are supposed to reach out and offer me some carpeted guidance.

Not to mention that having to interact with a whole other person is just annoying—meeting them, having them swab some impression of me, dealing with the whole exchange. It's like walking into a strange-smelling room of an old person's house and I don't *want* to.

So after I mentally throw myself through a plate-glass window about fifty times, I find myself studying him like you would an exotic animal. He apparently breathes air. The bottle of water on the table in front of him would point to a need for hydration. The pastel blue polo shirt he's wearing along with some khaki pants indicate his natural habitat is some sort of tech center (which was later confirmed).

He looks up and immediately puts his communication device down and then changes his mind and shoves it into his pocket. He stands and holds his hands up as if to show how big a fish was and says, "I'm Jim."

He looks like someone you would see trying to straighten out a picnic blanket.

I don't say anything. We stand there like some awkward triptych depicting people wearing the soft clothes of the twenty-first century. Finally Aaron says, "Hi, Jim. Thanks for coming. This is Jacob."

"Great!" Jim puts his hands in his pockets and rocks back on his heels in a friendly but sterile way. Aaron walks away. We sit down.

I put my arms on the table but find that the surface is too cold, so then I put them in my lap.

These are just some of the things I learned about Jim Dade, despite my deployment of steamrolling silence and catatonic stares, a technique that didn't faze him at all. He told me about himself as if he was checking off some sort of roster: "From Reston but grew up in Woodbridge. Went to Buchanan. Not one of those people who hated high school but didn't love it. Went to JMU in Harrisonburg. You been there? Great vegetarian restaurant. I, myself, am not vegetarian, though. Met Amy there, at JMU. That's my wife. Pregnant. Seven months. But we didn't marry then. Only when we met later at a singles get-together at the Jalapeno Café at Tyson's Corner mall. Tried online dating for a while. Wasn't my thing. I prefer human interaction to be more . . . analog. Eye contact. Now I work at Emtech. Even though I double-majored in computer science and history. I could have been a history teacher. But I work at Emtech."

The whole time he was talking he was bending and unbending a paper clip that he removed from his pants pocket as soon as we sat down. He methodically straightened it out and then bent it back to paper clip shape, then made a triangle, and finally a sort of spiral, all while talking at me robotically and not looking down.

Other observations: clean fingernails, short haircut suggests proclivity toward order while a slightly cushioned face points to a lack of exercise and probable access to a living room with satellite cable. Voice is monotone and punctuated by little shrugs indicating the kind of general ambivalence necessary to maintain a boring office job at tech center next to mega-furniture store in Reston.

I looked over and saw the shark's-tooth-necklace guy gesturing wildly. Jamie was shuffling his feet under the table like he was running away in his imagination.

Jim was talking and talking and then he stopped abruptly with "I'm an optimist." At which point I accidentally made eye contact with him and go, "Okay."

Jim Analysis

So this is what I could tell: Jim is basically a nice guy with the right American components of hard work and honesty. Jim is the kind of person who can manage emotions. All his emotions come in the right proportions and nothing is out of whack. I'm sure Jim has a well-functioning injustice barometer and would fight for a cause without too much hesitation, and if you happened to be in some bunker with him during a war, you wouldn't feel too weird telling him about your life. He would give you a pen if you needed it and then not ask for it back. Jim is the mail-opening, standing-in-line, car-owning diplomat from the bill-paying population that this juvenile detention center would like to insert me into after two more months.

Jim exists. Like some palatable form of technology. The question is not, is Jim good or bad? The question is not, do I want to be Jim? The question is, why do I have to meet with him for half an hour every Thursday afternoon in the cafeteria or, weather permitting, the courtyard? And also, what are we supposed to talk about?

Back to Our Meeting

So after I said, "Okay," I realized I had said one word too many. Jim leans back and points to his face and says, "Something else about me: history buff." I stared past him toward the empty snack racks at the end of the cafeteria.

"You have to go to school here, right? Are they teaching you a history"—he looked around—"unit?"

I sighed.

He goes, "Civics. I think that's what I remember taking in high school. A class called civics. And western civ."

He laughed.

I looked at the dirt under my fingernails.

"You getting any Civil War here? Any Vietnam? Nah...they're probably teaching you about the colonies, right? The Revolutionary War?

"I personally," he said, shifting in his seat, "am more into European history. Pre–World War One. Austro-Hungarian Empire, stuff like that. It's crazy, too. It's like"—and then he high-fived the air—"*fantasy.*"

"I mean, and then you've got Russia." He looked at me furtively. "Nicholas, Alexandra. Rasputin." He put his finger up in the air. "Whoa! Cue the record scratch. Wicked crazy monk.

"Anastasia," he said. "Little princess. Could be anywhere." He pinched his lip. "Well, but, that's been debunked, I think. Revolution. Lots of stuff burned."

Then, with his hand, he pantomimed quickly shaking some dice and throwing them on the table. "*Lenin.*

"But the thing is..." He leans forward, all business. "You never know what's true, what's fact, what's legend. I'm reading this book..." His voice trails off.

Then began the part of our meeting when Jim ran out of things to say and we sat in welling silence. We both shifted around and looked in different directions. I heard that lady talking to Denise behind me with a high, tinseled voice.

Jim's tactic for alleviating the awkwardness of sitting across from someone and not saying anything is to pretend to concentrate very hard on a succession of tiny missions. His first one was to furrow his brow and scratch furiously at a speck on the table. He then stared into the distance with a bemused expression on his face, as if he were trying to remember a funny incident. After that, he seemed to think there was something wrong with his chair, so he kept looking down and to the side and scooting it forward and then backward.

At one point I looked at Jim and he was staring at me with epic nostalgia, like my face was a paved-over rain forest. That made me uncomfortable. We both looked away. His phone rang and he silenced it.

He sat back and put the tips of his fingers together and said, "Well, this is weird."

Finally, he reached down and withdrew something kind of unwieldy from his briefcase. He goes, "I should probably let you go. But the counselor, Lane? Said that you like to draw?" He put a drawing pad and a clear plastic box with some fancy-looking pencils in it on the table. "So I got you these. Figured it might get kind of monotonous in here. Anyway, you don't have to use them, I just..." He trailed off.

He got up abruptly and said, "Well, nice meeting you, Jacob." And stuck out his hand like he wanted me to shake it. I didn't move. So then he goes, "Okay! See you next Thursday," and got his briefcase and left.

It's true. I do like to draw. But I don't know how Lane knows that.

Catalog of the Times I've Seen Andrea Since That Time in the Courtyard

Through the rec room window that looks out onto the hallway while we were emptying out trash cans. She was walking with her therapist, David Kittel.

At movie night last Friday. For some reason she wasn't at the one before. This time she was sitting in the opposite corner and we were late and it was dark and I didn't really get a good look at her.

Two days ago when I was being escorted to the bathroom and I saw her with the rest of the girls eating lunch in the cafeteria. She was sitting there staring at her food and not touching it, which is what *I* always do.

On her way out of the courtyard when we were being escorted in. Her cheeks were red as if she'd just run a long way. We totally made eye contact.

I guess that's about it.

But if my calculations prove correct, her batch of girls should overlap with my batch of guys in the computer room tomorrow. However, it will take some stealthy maneuvering to get to sit next to her. In order for that to happen, two things have to fall into place. First: the girls have to get there before the guys, which usually happens but not always. This would be optimal because that way I can make the decision to sit next to Andrea no matter which computer she's at, which brings me to the second thing, which is that no one else can decide to sit next to her. There is another factor, which is that assuming that we *do* get to sit next to each other, our level of interaction will depend on Mrs. Dandridge and how wrapped up she is in whatever stupid paperback she's reading. Sometimes she sculpts the atmosphere in the computer room with brooding, scalpel-edged glances.

And sometimes, if she's really into her book, she'll let things go a little and you can actually talk to someone.

Andrea Episode in Which We Make Fun of a Keyboard

It happened. I got to sit next to Andrea. Outcome: a new rung has been reached on whatever relationship/friendship ladder it is that ultimately leads to doing it.

When we got to the computer room, the girls were ahead of us and standing in line at Mrs. Dandridge's desk, signing honor slips. Andrea was toward the front, bobbing up and down in place like she had to pee or something. She signed the piece of paper and then flung it into the plastic tray and turned around and walked to computer number five, which is next to a spiky potted plant and at the end of the middle row.

So then it was just a matter of whether or not someone else was going to sit next to her. I did the math of how many people there were in front of me and how many computers were left and it seemed like a pretty slim chance the seat wouldn't be taken by the time I got up there. Then again, everyone knows the keyboard at computer number four is totally fucked. It's covered in a thick protective plastic sheath that is too small. So whenever you push down a key, it pushes down five other keys, and it takes you like, ten minutes to type one word because you have to delete so many times.

At one point, Eddie Alvarez went over there and looked like he was about to sit down, but he decided against it and sat at computer number one in the first row.

As I was standing in line, I was also trying to assess the atmosphere of the room, trying to feel how limber it was. When Dandridge is really into a book, she'll let the level of talking bubble up to that of maybe a waiting room or coffee shop and it's possible to have a quiet conversation.

I was hoping she'd still be reading *Skygate,* which she's been pretty engrossed in lately. Sure enough, when I got up there, she had it open and was even tracing along the words with her engorged finger. When she saw it was me, however, she did what she usually does, which is to make a big elaborate show of putting her bookmark in her book, closing it, placing it on the desk, crossing her hands and watching my every move. But this time she did it more distractedly, and when I was done signing in, she went right back to reading.

I turned around, ready for the computer room to bear the fruits of my labor, when I noticed that Andrea wasn't there anymore. As I got closer, I saw she was under the desk, messing with some cords. I sat at the computer next to hers and looked around to see if anyone else noticed. Then I leaned down and said, "What are you doing?" She bumped her head on the table and looked over her shoulder and I'm pretty sure her face softened when she saw it was me. She said, "Trying to untangle this extension cord. I keep hitting it with my foot."

I was like, "Nice."

She messed with it for a few more minutes while I tried to log on to computer number four. Finally she came up and breathed in like she was gulping for air. She pushed some hair out of her face. I looked back at Mrs. Dandridge. She was glued to her book. Denise Henly and Jamie Perkins were whispering to each other in the corner.

I knew I had to say something at the very beginning or else a scab of silence would form that would last through the half hour. So I breathed in and was like, "I...," but then I realized that I didn't have anything to say and it was like jumping off a diving board only to realize the pool was empty and I was plummeting toward the concrete floor while simultaneously watching all my planning disintegrate, when Andrea goes, "This space bar sticks."

She was pounding it with her finger over and over again.

I go, "I know!" a little too loudly. Then I said, "This plastic thing is the worst, though," referring to the sheath covering my keyboard. "It's like, impossible to type."

She goes, "I know. I've had that computer before. It's like, you try to type and you can't, because it's impossible."

I go, "Impossible."

It was here that I started to think about where I could insert what I consider to be the secret weapon in my arsenal of anecdotes. It's a little story that has the three-pronged effect of making me seem dangerous, tragic, and kind of thoughtful. It's about how when I was a kid, I was so sick of listening to my mom and her then-boyfriend fight that I got really high, fell out of a window, and watched an ant stumble back and forth across the hairs on my arm and thought about how maybe I should be a farmer.

I looked around. A few other people were talking. Eddie Alvarez was exaggeratedly shrugging his shoulders. The JDC homepage on my computer was frozen.

I'm usually pretty good at sculpting conversations for personal effect; kind of veering them toward some self-deprecating exchange that conveys how great or wounded or smart I am.

I go, "These computers are so old they remind me of the like, *first* computer. I remember once going to a CompUSA with my friend's parents back when I lived in Texas."

This was meant to give Andrea an opening to ask me about myself. I feel like anyone else would have responded, "Oh, you lived in Texas, wow, let me go down on you." But what actually happened was she resumed banging on her spacebar. She goes, "I wish this keyboard would get struck by lightning."

I continued. "Yeah, it was really, really cold in there. And there were all these bulky computers like, remember how everything used to be kind of boxy and bulky?"

She was still messing with the keyboard, banging on it with her thumb and then holding it down. Her screen shuddered and flashed. I looked back at Dandridge, who licked the tip of one of her disgusting fingers and then turned the page of her book.

Andrea goes, "I wish this keyboard would get stuck in a perpetual cycle of spousal abuse."

I laughed. I didn't even mean to or think I was going to. But suddenly it was like a gust of wind had lifted the hat off my head and was twirling it in the sky and I was laughing.

I was like, "Yeah, I wish I could put it on the Trail of Tears." She laughed. Not as hard as I did, but still. A strand of hair fell across her face and she brushed it away.

She goes, "But I know what you mean about other people's parents" (even though I hadn't really said anything about other people's parents). "My best friend in eighth grade — her parents didn't like me. They were the most typical parents, like they were grown on some parent plantation or something where everyone wears sweaters. They had these old photographs all lined up in their living room, but you could tell they weren't really old. And they thought they were so awesome because they had some crinkled photographs in their hallway, even though you know they were just made to look that way on a computer. You know what I mean?"

"Yeah."

"Anyway. They didn't like me. They always looked at me like I was a smudge."

I knew exactly what she meant by that, too. I knew what

she meant really, really hard. I wanted to put my fingers in her mouth. But I just said, "I know what you mean."

Then BAM! we were in this conversation about other people's parents and what it's like when they don't like you. Which is something I'd never really talked about, but I had so much to say. I didn't even care that I didn't get to tell my anecdote; I even forgot about it because there was all this other stuff to say. We might as well have been at the beach or sitting on top of a slide. I didn't even notice when computer time was over.

Talk Times

Okay so Andrea and I have been having conversations. Like real, not boring, information trading and analyzing, blasted with laughs, revelatory conversations where time warps and it's like we have day passes to each other's souls. I've never really been able to talk to anyone like that except for Rocky, and that was only a few times.

We don't get to see each other that often. Only in the courtyard when her batch of girls gets in rotation with my batch of guys. And on movie nights. And sometimes in the computer room. But when we do see each other, we'll sit down and get through these preliminary sifting questions really quick and suddenly I'm telling her shit that I didn't even know I thought. I'm talking like some updated, more advanced version of myself like Jacob 7.0 for the new world or something and then she comes in with her own thing, her own monologue with all of its undertones of previous jokes and reference points that we both have and she's touching her face and talking faster and we're circling around jokes and then making them and she'll take it up a notch and make it funnier and then it's like we're ripping the filling out of everything. It's like we're on some jokey houseboat where the whole world is accidentally getting dragged up behind us.

And then all the anger, all the resentment I feel that day knocking around inside me like sneakers in a washing machine, it stops. It gets put on hold or filed away and I can almost feel like a person who doesn't usually feel that way, and if I did at one point, now it's gone, and that's okay, too. I'm like, noticing that one of her eyeballs doesn't quite track the other and staring at her haystacks of eyelashes. And even though I'm talking way more than I usually do, it's the most quiet I've ever felt.

Things I Have Noticed About Andrea

She slouches a lot. When she reaches up to put her hair back you can tell what she's going to look like when she gets older. Her fingernails are always dirty. The insides of her wrists are lighter than the outsides. She has a slight southern accent. She holds one of her elbows with the other hand when she's thinking about something. She seems pretty bored all the time but then when you say something good her face will break open and she'll consider you like you are a sunny rock bed. Sometimes she'll be staring off into space as if she's transfixed by something in her head and she'll literally snap out of it. She licks her lips when she's about to say something. She's got a small scar on the inside of her right eyebrow. One of her shoes is always untied. She does pretty good impressions of people here, like Pastor Todd and her therapist, David Kittel. And when she's doing one and she's especially into it, it's like she busts a seam and you can sense this boundless energy. You can tell when she's just washed her hair, because it suddenly has all these shiny planes in it. If there was some postapocalyptic situation where to survive everyone had to reveal who they really were, Andrea would probably be really quiet at first and then emerge as a leader because she's good at making net assessments about the way things really *are*. She smells like pollen. Sometimes she'll take one eyelid and just hold it closed. In the category of being where you're just waiting, like in line or something, Andrea always seems like she's waiting for some big and really universal change. You can feel the depth of her waiting like you can feel the depth of a well by throwing a penny down it. She looks slightly different every time I see her. She has really thick eyelashes. Sometimes she'll make a little animal gesture, like turn her head really quickly to look at something, and I'll feel like I recognize her from an ancient time. Some of her teeth are whiter than her other teeth. Once, in the computer room, I saw her smell the eraser at the end of a pencil after she'd used it.

I wonder if she's a virgin. Or maybe she's really sexually aggressive. Or maybe she's had sex just a few times. I wonder if she masturbates in her room and what she thinks of. And if she comes easily or it takes a while or she never does. She doesn't seem like she never does.

It's like I think about her all the time. Like every moment has a little pupil of Andrea. I knocked my toothbrush off my sink the other day and the sound it made when it clattered to the floor reminded me of her. There were patches of water drying on the courtyard today and they reminded me of her, too.

Sometimes when she's talking I want to put all my fingers in her mouth and pull her wider. I want to like, turn her inside out and look at all the folds. I want her to be a series of stacked-up blocks that will come tumbling down over me.

It's not even about sex. I mean I obviously want to put my dick in her but I also want to crash into her like a berg that she has to accommodate with her whole being. I want to reach up inside her and grab some essence, some liquid distillation of her laugh and smile and lather myself with it like in a commercial for soap.

"We need to find a dusty dome," she said. This was yesterday. We were sitting in the cafeteria, at the very back, against the large glass window that looks out onto the hallway. Sometimes the JDC has guest speakers come and talk to us about things like "Decision Making" or "Conflict Resolution." The pro is that you get to leave class for a while. The con is that you have to sit and listen to some handout-happy dickface proselytize about making "Life Tabs." Today's session was about "Organization." Upon entering the cafeteria, we each received a packet that I hadn't looked at yet but that was sure to contain a number of bullet points.

"To sit on and watch the sunset," she continued. We were talking about being the last two people on earth. Everyone was facing the front of the cafeteria, talking or rocking back and forth. Pastor Todd was in the corner, glancing around furtively. Aaron and Jake were at the front of the room. The guest speaker was late.

"And maybe there will be some horses."

"Yeah," I said. "I'll have some sort of pack, with stuff that I got from a convenience store. We'll eat whatever's in it."

"Yeah, we can think of all the Fourth of Julys that happened. Or we could even pretend it was the Fourth of July, since we would be the only people left, whatever we said would just go."

"Yeah, we could like, designate everything."

"We could make all our clothes out of flannel."

"And collect a bunch of Bubble Wrap."

"Totally," she said. "I'd probably eat a lot of graham crackers." She pulled on her earlobe. "The only thing that might suck is that I'd never get to visit Stonehenge."

Lane walked into the cafeteria, checked her watch and conferred with Pastor Todd. She jutted her elbow out and removed what must have been a hair from under her arm and let it waft to the ground. Then they stopped talking and idly searched the room in a way that made me realize they might not like each other very much.

Andrea was digging her fingernail under the staple in her packet. "We could imagine all of those families on all of those Fourth of Julys on all of those damp blankets, and how all of it was leading up to *this*."

"Everything crumbling and empty."

"Like a busted snow globe," she said.

"No more moments. No more four-year-olds with the reflection of fireworks on their eyeballs."

"Right," she said. "No more worried moms struggling with screen windows."

"No more overly air-conditioned electronics stores."

"Or hearing a recording of your voice and thinking it doesn't sound like yourself," she said. "I hate that.

"You know what?" She leaned toward me. "I just thought of this. I had a friend who worked at the BlueStar Pavilion last summer. It's this pavilion outside of Staunton where they have bands play and stuff. She showed me how to get into the shell, like, the stage, even though it's usually locked. And where the lighting board is and everything. We would go there at night sometimes, when there wasn't an event, and sneak in."

She was talking like her unalloyed, slightly embarrassing, skidding-off-the-tracks self; her purest, most Andrea-est element.

"We could do that," she said. "Once we're both out of here. You could come to Staunton and we could sneak into the pavilion. It's easy. We can go there at night and turn all the lights on and sit in the shell and pretend we're the last two people on earth."

"Yes," I said, looking at her straight in the eyes.

The guest speaker finally arrived. She was carrying a leather portfolio and yet more handouts. She was flushed and apologetic as she spoke to Aaron. And then she turned and gave us this sweeping gaze, as if we were an ocean.

"Tell me something," said Andrea, "that you've never told anyone."

"Okay," I said. "I can't swim."

Sunday

Beans came to visit today. I didn't know we were allowed to have random visitors, but I guess we are on Sundays. I had just finished wiping down the windows in the common room for chore time and was sitting on my bed and writing in this notebook when Officer O'Connell shows up. He goes, "Son, your mom's here." I go, "Beans?" "I guess." We walk to the cafeteria, and there she is, sitting at a table, wearing a button-down shirt where one half is white and the other half is peach-colored.

I sit down across from her and notice her hair is different. It's shorter and full of curls that look wet and crispy at the same time and it's all slung over to one side. Her hands are crossed on the table. This time with little palm trees painted on each of her fingernails.

She's sitting still, not fidgeting like last time. And instead of doing her usual thing of darting her eyes around nervously, her face is as calm as a pond.

"Jake," she says and quickly touches my elbow. She leans forward. "How *are* you?" Her voice—that's different, too. Different and familiar at the same time. There's marrow in it that I'd never heard before.

I shrugged my shoulders. "I dunno," I said. I felt disoriented, sitting across from her right then. I go, "Why are you *here?*" But it came out sounding way meaner than I meant it to.

She paused for a moment. "Well, I thought, you know. It's Sunday."

It's Sunday. As if any day of the week has ever been any impetus to do anything before.

"Yeah," I said. "Sunday."

"I want to show you something," she said, looking around in her purse. She withdrew a photograph and put it on the table and turned it sideways so we both could see it. It depicted a bunch of humans in front of a building, squinting into the sun. There was a row of old people in wheelchairs, and then behind them, a row of women linking arms.

"It's at the Twin Oaks Senior Center," said my mom. "I went there with some of the girls from work and we did their hair for free. It's part of a program they have going there." I looked at the photograph and had a hard time identifying my mom at first. Finally I found her. She was leaning over to say something to the person next to her and they both looked like they were about to burst out laughing.

"Which person's hair did you do?" I said.

"Well, you can't really see her," said my mom. "She's over here, in the corner." She pointed with one of her shiny nails. "She was real sweet. She just wanted a basic frost." My mom shook her head and smiled at the photograph.

I looked around the cafeteria. There was a little paper-product city set up on one of the folding tables next to the empty salad bar—stacks of napkins, towers of cups.

She adjusted some bracelets on her wrist. "I finally found something I like to do," she said. She put her hands up slowly and patted the air like she was feeling a wall in the dark. The bangles made a tinkling sound as they slid down her arm. Then she said cautiously, as if she were discovering each word as she went along, "I like . . . to . . . touch . . . people's . . . hair."

I had no idea how to react to this.

She laughed a sunny laugh and then pushed the photograph toward me. "Keep it," she said.

I slowly pulled the photograph over. Usually my mom is a photocopy of herself printed out on sandpaper. But today she was in color, normal, shifting around in the confines of her own noonday box of sober thought.

"Listen," she said, leaning forward. "I don't want to keep you for too much longer. But there's something else I wanted to tell you, the reason I came here today." And for the first time during our meeting the veneer of confidence left her. "I've left Steve. I mean it this time. The girls are helping me with the paperwork and everything."

She was looking at me to see how I would react. She's "left" Refrigerator Man "for good" a bunch of times. Somehow, he always manages to heave back into our lives. I decided to be as still as I could possibly be. More still than a broken flashlight at the bottom of a cave. More still than a bubble in the mottled glass window of a historical house.

"You okay, kiddo?" She was squinting at me.

"Yeah," I managed to croak out.

"I don't expect you to believe me this time, of all the times," said my mom, swirling her hand in the air. "Why would you? I understand that. But I've *made* a decision." She dug her fingernails into her chest. "Anyway," she said, sitting back, seemingly exhausted.

Before she left I looked at the photograph again. The women all looked really capable, the way they were smiling and squinting in different directions and casually leaning on the wheelchairs. And my mom, she seemed so normal, like she could have been part of any drift of happy women.

Condor Court II

Like I said before, all the streets were named after birds of prey and our favorite house was on Condor Court.

It was really quiet out there, but if you listened hard you could hear world static. Like when you put your ear to a seashell.

Other than that, you could sometimes hear the breeze pushing along some plastic sheeting. We spent so much time in the house on Condor Court because it was the biggest and the most finished. It had actual curtains and shit. It had a giant cardboard entertainment center so whatever dickface family was going to move in could see how it would look with all of their electronics. It had white wall-to-wall carpeting, even on the stairs.

It had a big kitchen with deep, gleaming sinks, and an empty pool outside that scarred your eyes with brightness on sunny days. In the bathroom of the master bedroom were two gigantic mirrors facing each other, reflecting an infinite army of lined-up yous when you stood between them. It had a wide staircase and marble floors and many lacquered and shiny surfaces. It was all new carpet and clean house cartilage and quietness and light. Except for when you rang the doorbell, which sounded like the sound track to a flower opening in slow motion.

We could get out onto the roof from one of the bathroom windows, and you could see the whole empty neighborhood from there. All the front doors with gold-plated address numbers on them and stone walkways. Everything looked like it had been gingerly placed there and a strong gust of wind could blow it all away.

On a decorative table at the foot of the stairs was a large vase filled with blue glass pebbles. We would grab handfuls and fling them into the pool from the deck, trying to hit the drain.

One afternoon we were sitting in the living room. Rocky was

flinging blue glass pebbles into the fireplace. I was watching a square of light edge up the cardboard entertainment center and welling in a hole we'd burned through it with a lighter the day before. We were spreading out in the silence of another off-road afternoon in the empty house. He would fling the pebbles so they'd clatter against the brick and sometimes ping off the little brass fence. Sometimes they would bounce off a dark steel container that held pokers and was meant to look like a dog detective. He threw one and it hit something in the fireplace, something that we couldn't see, with a papery thud. I didn't think anything of it, but Rocky went to see what it was.

He came back to the couch holding something rolled up in newspaper. He sat down next to me and started opening it. He had to hold it up and shake it and let it unfold itself, and when he did, something fell onto his lap. It was a plastic bag like you would use for a sandwich. It was foggy, and the bottom was lined with white powder. Rocky picked it up and let it dangle in the air. We stared at it for the longest time. And then we looked at each other. And then we looked around the living room kind of quickly as if we'd never seen it before. The thing about danger is that it makes you feel *enclosed*.

Condor Court III

After we found the Baggie in the fireplace, we sat there for a while. I had the feeling someone was watching us. I wanted to leave. Rocky held it in his hands and kept lifting it up and down like he was weighing it.

"Where do you think it comes from?" he said.

"I don't know... one of the construction workers maybe."

"Yeah, probably."

Rocky looked at it close, then started pinching different parts with his fingers. I looked at the newspaper, now on the floor. Part of it said "¿Puedo caminar?"

"What do you think we should do with it?"

"I don't know," I said. I leaned back and stretched, trying to seem casual. But even though I was just a kid, I knew that it wasn't the kind of thing someone would forget about. I felt strange looking at it. Like I had accidentally walked into the wrong wing of a cold museum.

The square of light had moved up the entertainment center and now illuminated a bunch of fake buttons and dials on the fake stereo.

"Do you think we should try it?"

I started laughing. I don't know why I started laughing. Rocky started laughing too. He had a birthmark on his neck shaped like a bottle. Sometimes when he was excited, a vein under it would bulge out a little. I thought of our skateboards outside, lying in the grass, baking in the sun.

I go, "Fuck, yeah."

"Where?" he said.

"Where what?"

"Where should we do it?"

"Oh. The kitchen," I said definitively.

The kitchen table was glass—a huge disk placed on an antique-looking iron stand. Rocky flung the bag down on it and walked away as if he'd done this a million times.

"Where are you going?" I said.

"Nothing," he said and turned around and walked back.

We stared at the bag.

"Now what do we do?" I said.

"Duh. We snort it."

"Oh, yeah. Duh."

"Duh."

"Okay," said Rocky. He leaned over and picked up the bag and opened it a tiny bit, just enough to let a little powder through. Then he opened it a little more and tried to coax the powder, shaking it gently. And then a bunch avalanched out onto the table.

"Wow," I said. At that point, I really wanted to go home.

Rocky leaned over it. "How do we..."

"I've got it," I said. I shoved my hand into my front pocket and withdrew a dollar bill along with two dirty pennies and some cellophane wrappers. I laid the bill out on the table and tried to roll it up, but it was so sweaty and old that I ended up crushing it.

"It's too flimsy," said Rocky. "We need a crisp dollar bill."

"Crisp!" I said. And then I karate-chopped the air with my hand. I was already feeling a little different.

Rocky: "Maybe we can just...," and takes one of the cellophane wrappers and tries to straighten it out and shape it into a little canoe. Then he actually pinches some of the powder with his fingers and drops it into the wrapper. Except most of it just stuck to him, and the little that did fall into the wrapper bounced around and jumped off because he couldn't keep it still.

"Crud." He wiped his hands on his shirt.

"I've got it," I said, and ran out of the kitchen and into the dining room where the table was all set for dinner. Sunlight illuminated the upended leather couch. I saw, for the first time, what a mess we'd made — the torn-out light fixture, scattered pieces of fake ice, broken side tables and wineglasses. I grabbed one of the knives off the table and ran back into the kitchen.

"Gimme it," Rocky said when he saw it. I gave it to him and he managed to herd some of the powder onto it. He wiped his hands on his jeans and then held the knife out to me.

I go, "You want me to go first?"

He goes, "You got the knife."

"Oh, yeah, that logic is airtight."

"Fine," he says and withdraws.

I'm like, "No, no, just give it to me."

He hands me the knife and some of it spills off. In my head I was like, "Oh shit, oh shit, oh shit." I felt like I was walking a plank. I leaned over, closed one of my nostrils, and sniffed in. When I came up, Rocky was looking at me like I was really far away. Like I was a horizon and he was waiting to see if a ship was going to appear.

"Why are you looking at me like that?" I said.

"Like what?"

"Like I'm about to go crazy."

"You're not," he said. "I mean, I'm not."

"You still are."

"Did it hurt?" he said.

"No. I mean, yeah. It's like a cold burn."

At first I didn't feel anything, but then my cheeks got warm and my heart started beating faster and a waterfall of words started coming out of my mouth. "Then Mrs. Pruitt comes over and busts me for drawing on her desk like it's the Constitution and how could anyone ever draw on it and she took away my pencil like it was some sort of mystical baton and I'd never be able to get another one not in a million years..."

I picked up a fake pear from the fruit bowl on the table and started tossing it back and forth and shrugging at the same time. I felt like a surly chipmunk umpire.

"But yeah he's sort of a dick but I mean he's not that bad but he can be sort of an idiot most of the time and he always calls me Jake and is like, 'Jake, that's for *home* use...'"

My eyes had been fixed on the bright rim of the pool outside the sliding glass door. I wanted to hear the electronic chimes of the doorbell. I looked at Rocky who was clutching his chest and white-knuckling the back of a chair.

"You okay?"

"Heart murmur," he said.

"What?"

"Heart. Murmur. I have one. And I think this shit is tangling it up even more and giving me a heart attack."

"Follow me," I said.

The doorbell to the front door was encased in a bronze diamond-shaped fixture. I told Rocky to just stand there and then I pushed it a bunch of times. For a moment we were transfixed by the unfurling synthetic chimes. They spun a cocoon of sound around us and it seemed to calm Rocky down. Then we busted out of the cocoon and went up onto the roof to look at the neighborhood.

It was empty. Deserted. Shuddering with silence. But the sky was all big above us, the sun like a crash symbol being hit over and over again, shedding brightness. I had this feeling and even as I was having it I knew it was a different kind of feeling—I suddenly saw where we were: a zygote-dwelling place gouged out of the Texas plains, sterilized and new with its glass and layers of creeping light. I saw how everyone, with their synchronized good intentions, would gather here and wait. And I also felt, sweepingly, like the way you sometimes feel at the end of a movie, how *temporary* it all was. I looked down. My knuckles were bloody from scraping them on the roof, which I didn't even know I was doing. I gazed back out across the neighborhood, and it was the first time I really saw it.

We then got the cardboard entertainment center from the living room and lugged it down to the backyard and tried to set it on fire in the empty pool. It didn't really work, so we went up to the master bedroom and jumped on the mattress for a while.

Rocky took the cover off and draped it over his head and started running around in circles until he slammed into the closet door. I pulled a seashell-shaped air freshener out of the wall, put it on my head, and did some slow-motion karate moves between the two mirrors in the bathroom. That really cracked Rocky up.

I finally fell down on the cover that Rocky had left rumpled on the floor. It had a pattern of pastel sunsets on it. I remember thinking it was the most pleasing collection of colors I had ever seen. Then I went to sleep. Or actually I just lay there for a while with my body thrumming like I was a plucked guitar string.

Later, feeling empty and damp, we took the Baggie and buried it in a large bowl of fake fruit in the kitchen, covering it with airbrushed apples and pears. We couldn't really make eye contact. I had this feeling that I was bruised somewhere, or that I had bruised something else, like accidentally rolled over a baby bird in bed. I was thirsty so I went into the living room and got one of the wineglasses and took it to the kitchen sink but when I turned on the faucet, nothing came out. Rocky was bent over, tying his shoe. Finally we were both like, "See you tomorrow." But we didn't go back to the development for a few days. And both of us pretended to forget where the Baggie was hidden.

Another Meeting with Jim

I have a feeling that Jim Dade, bearer of paper clips, has never been late for anything in his entire life. He was sitting at the round table this afternoon when Officer O'Connell escorted me to the perpetually frigid rec room (the cafeteria was being used for a luncheon and it was raining, so that ruled out the courtyard) in what was to be our second meeting.

I sat down across from him. He sat forward and made a

parenthesis with his hands and said, "Haircut." Indeed, his hair was shorter.

He was wearing khakis and a slightly different pastel polo shirt. He had his paper clip out, and there was a book on the table in front of him. It had a filmy plastic cover and said *Our Galaxy*.

"So how have your last two weeks been?"

I couldn't muster enough hostility to meet this question with complete silence. But I didn't want to *say* anything either because I'm not trying to lay the groundwork for some tale of an inspiring mentor/juvenile relationship where we both spark separate revelations in each other's lives and eventually realize he needed me as much as I needed him and then bound off into our happy, product-laden futures. So I take it upon myself to just shrug.

Jim goes, "Uh-huh. Yeah. I hear ya, I hear ya."

He catches me looking at the book and goes, "*Our Galaxy*. Got it at the library. From the seventies. Crazy space pictures. Thought you might like it."

He turned to a page that showed an artist's conception of what a satellite planet of Jupiter might look like. It had craggy ice mountains rising from the ocean and a crapload of stars in the background.

Jim's like, "Crazy, huh?

"Anyway," he says, "it's yours. Well, actually it's from the library so you have to give it back. But you can keep it for a while."

At that point the low hum from the air vents stopped suddenly, landing us in unnerving silence. We both looked around.

"My wife, Amy?" Jim continued. "She wants to repaint the living room. I said, 'Why don't we paint a mural of this picture?' and she said, 'We already decided to paint it Topaz Mist.' I said, 'Topaz Mist?' She said, 'Yeah, Topaz Mist.'"

My head had slid off my palm and was inching down my arm and I had to jolt myself awake before it hit the table.

I was really tired this afternoon. I felt drunk. As soon as my body found a comfortable arrangement in the plastic chair, my brain would fall away like an egg yolk slipping off a spoon. I'd come to, shift my weight, and rest my head on my other hand, and unintentionally listen to what Jim was saying for a moment before going under again.

Anyone else with a catatonic person in front of them in a freezing room full of beige would not consider the situation to be one that was fertile for conversation. But if my drooling on the table made him uncomfortable, he certainly didn't make it obvious.

As far as I can tell, after he was finished talking about Amy, he spent the next fifteen minutes of our meeting talking about work ("Oh, man. Chrissie. Our new receptionist. Nice lady, but man did she mess up payroll. So since I'm the only other person who knows how to do it, I had to walk her through the whole process. Then I found out that the whole part-swapping department was three weeks behind . . ."), bending and unbending the paper clip. Later he would start to push his cuticles down with it, a detail that felt uncomfortably intimate to witness, like smelling someone's bad breath.

When I started listening again, snagged into consciousness by a sudden shrill beep from the smoke detector, Jim was talking about JFK. From what I can understand, sparked by an article or a book a friend gave him or something, Jim is now in the midst of an obsession with the Kennedy assassination containing notes of desperation that can only make me wonder what is missing in his home life.

He described to me, in what seemed like unnecessarily minute detail, each of the nine prevalent conspiracy theories surrounding the president's death. He was like, "There are a *lot* of badly formatted conspiracy websites out there."

When excited about a subject, Jim's usual staccato talking

style of short, bullet-point sentences expands into oceanic mono-logues.

"It's like a large, papier mâché ball," he said. I believe this par-ticular tangent was emboldened by the fact that I accidentally made eye contact with him.

"Composed of bits of faded, stuck-together paper, so many theories and countertheories."

He's grabbing the table like he's about to fling it over. And it became apparent that he had collected all these facts and needed to air-guitar with them for a while:

"And each milky bit of paper could contain something impor-tant, something that you don't want to *forget*. There are so many conflicting overlapping facts, so much evidence that points to different universes of possibility. You keep trying to think of it in the right way, but in order to do so, all of these different planes have to be coordinated, all of these dimensions in place. And one dimension obscures the other. The world changes with each new theory. Each new idea indicates different motivations, gov-ernments poised in different directions of evil; different inter-pretations of what the *air* was like that morning.

"There's just so much information, such a freight of suspicion, that you look at it all and you think, There's no way anyone could get to the bottom of all of this. And maybe all you can do is *interpret* what happened. Take all the information and sculpt it into something that fits your idea of the world. But which one is right? Which one is true? Which one is an accurate picture of *what happened?*"

It was then that, despite my best efforts, I found myself stuck in a conversation with him.

What happened was that I was dozing off when I sensed a creeping silence. I looked up and Jim was staring at me with epic nostalgia again. Without meaning to I go, "*What?*"

He snaps out of it and goes, "Nothing. You remind me of someone. My brother."

I pause. "Okay."

Jim sits back. He sits forward and distractedly traces one of the letters of the galaxy book with his paper clip.

He's like, "Where did you say you went to high school? Potomac?"

It's quiet for a second as I decide whether to answer or not. Finally I go, "East."

"East?"

"Potomac."

"East Potomac?"

"Yeah."

Then, for some reason, I continued talking. It was like I was on a merry-go-round I couldn't stop.

I go, "And Wilson."

Jim sits forward, "What?"

"Wilson Secondary. I also went there. After I got kicked out of Robert E. Lee."

I looked at the table. I was afraid that Jim was going to have muted triumph in his eyes, like he finally got me to say something. But he was actually staring past me like he was thinking of something completely different.

He glanced at me and then picked up his paper clip and said, "Yeah. That's funny. East Potomac. That's where Ely went. I went to Buchanan, up in Falls Church. Zoning laws changed, though. So by the time Ely was ready to go to school, he had a choice. Parents thought he'd be better at Potomac."

The smoke detector beeped again.

"I used to pick him up after school," Jim continued. "In front of the gas station across the street? He always stole candy."

I pictured automatic doors and cold, sterile aisles.

"It's a pharmacy now," I said. "PVC Drug."

"Really?" Jim laughed and sat back.

"Yeah."

"'Regular People. Regular Prices,'" he said.

Then neither of us knew what to say.

Officer O'Connell finally showed up to escort me back to my room. Jim gave him a good-natured nod of acknowledgment. We both stood up, noisily pushing back our chairs. There was this awkward moment where Jim was like, "Oh, yeah, those pencils and sketch pad. Have they been working out for you?"

I had to say something because they were both looking at me, waiting for me to tie off the situation so we could all get on with the next thing.

"They were confiscated." Which they were. Aaron had taken them away and said I could use them during free time if I came and asked him which I hadn't done yet. Even though I've been thinking about it.

Jim goes, "Oh," and looked down at his hands.

I felt kind of bad. "But he said I could maybe still use them sometime."

"That's great!" The fault line of despair in his soul having apparently been sutured.

That's pretty much all that happened. The only thing different is, this time when Jim stuck his hand out for me to shake it, I did. I also took the book.

Jim Analysis II

Okay, so Jim is this twenty-first-century person who has figured out how to operate at a life tempo that is not destructive and has actually seemed to secure him some variety of contentment. I mean, I sense the regular-person restlessness I think everyone has (hence the Kennedy shit). It's not like he's a robot. But the way he carries himself, it's like he's the good-natured operator of a tiny unimpressive domain. I wonder what his moments are like. Like, when he's waiting in an elevator or adjusting a watch on his wrist; like, how many parts despair, how many parts optimism, how many parts just cruising on autopilot, how many parts bobbing in the past.

Of all the different varieties of all the different ways a person can be there's the way he is. And of all the collapsing and regenerating outcomes from the choices he's made, he's managed to secure what he calls a "pretty standard duplex" next to a mega-furniture store. And a job at Emtech.

He's aware of the obligations that compose his life and he doesn't resent them. He doesn't traffic in tiny perceived victories over other people like Refrigerator Man does. He doesn't float through life on an inner tube of margaritas and easy breaks, not caring how many people he fucks over in the process, like Malibu Mike did. He seems to be oriented toward some North Star of responsibility he thinks will make him happy. Or maybe he doesn't think so and he acts that way anyway.

He's the kind of person who if you were standing in line and the checkout person messed up and was causing everyone to wait wouldn't freak out or make a big deal out of it, or even shift and sigh loudly to convey his irritation. He would stand there and all of his internal machinations about the situation would be tempered by his belief that everyone is pretty much trying to do their best.

So here's this variety of nice guy. Here's the prototype of a good person. But I still don't really understand what the like, undertow of his intentions is; what everything he does is based on. Is it the desire to minimize pain? To find happiness? Or to be helpful? Is he adding to something or taking away from it? And also — is that way, the way Jim is, the way I'm supposed to be?

In Which Andrea and I Basically Have Sex

So Andrea and I basically had sex today. Okay not really. We didn't even kiss. But in a way, we kind of fucked. I mean, without even using our privates. But if the definition of *fucking* is to wetly traverse some hump of intimacy then we definitely did that.

I had kind of been feeling like something was going to happen with us because we were getting to that level of mutual attraction where it was like standing on the edge of a pool with your toes over the edge and you're having that debate with yourself about when to dive in. But there's no *place* to dive in here, especially when you're constantly being monitored by policemen, authority figures, little cameras, and the occasional nurse. There's free time, but that's when you're separated off into your rooms and are required to have the door open.

So it's pretty impossible to find even one square inch of privacy, *except*, that is, in the rec room on movie nights. I know this only through tons of trial and error. Everyone is supposed to sit on the floor and watch the television that is set up in front of the whiteboard. Officer O'Connell is there, usually sitting in the back so he can see what's going on. There is one corner, however, that's out of his line of vision because it's cloaked by the shadow of the door and next to a huge plastic trash can. Basically, everything has to align the right way. But if the door is at this specific angle and the trash can is in a certain place, a small area is created where two people can sit unobserved against the wall. So it's not exactly a motel room but it's better than nothing.

That's where Andrea and I always sit. Her with her chin resting on her knees and me Indian-style. We'll usually make fun of whatever movie we're watching or whisper about something else. Last night was different, though. We sat down and didn't say anything. It's like we *both* knew that something was going to happen.

Officer O'Connell got up and messed with the DVD player and finally got it to work. Then he turned the lights off and sat down. Me and Andrea still hadn't said anything to each other, and instead of having her knees under her chin, she was sitting with her legs straight and hands resting in her lap.

The movie was apparently about sick people who learn to live again or some shit, because whenever I looked at it, there was an old person in a hospital gown spinning around in a wheelchair. But I wasn't really paying attention. I was more listening to Andrea's breath and watching her hands. She seemed strangely still and wooden. I'm not positive, but I'm pretty sure that she wasn't paying attention to the movie either.

I started to get this feeling like I had to do something or my brain was going to short-circuit. I looked at Officer O'Connell. He was dozing in his chair. I looked around the room. Everyone was in the same restless state of not knowing how to sit and shifting around and being kind of bored. Then, without even really thinking about it, I took Andrea's hand and held it in mine. It was really warm. I thought I heard her quickly breathe in. We both continued staring straight ahead.

I held her hand for a little while and then brought it over to rest on my leg. I pushed my thumb into her damp palm harder and harder because I wanted to see when it would hurt. I wanted her to react. She shifted and exhaled. I loosened my grip. I quickly looked at her face—the eruption of softness that is her lips. I wanted to put my whole arm down her mouth and have it rest in the wet room of her body.

On the television a woman was running through a maze of shrubs. Andrea started kneading my leg. At that point I had a boner that must have been harder than the side of a ship. And I could barely fathom the possibility of what was about to happen as her hand edged up my leg, pushing the material of my sweatpants up with it. My hand was still covering hers and I couldn't tell who was guiding who and my heart was beating really fast and who knows what would have happened if Desean Phillips hadn't knocked into the trash can on his way to the bathroom. It wobbled and resettled in a different position. Officer O'Connell looked in our direction. Andrea snatched her hand away.

We sat like normal for a while, completely still. Maybe things would have started up again if the movie hadn't ended, but it did. When we got up to leave, right before she turned away to go with the girls, she whispered into my hair—into the hair that covers my ears, "Now I'm all slimy." At first I didn't really know what she was talking about. Like, it didn't hit me what she meant. But then it did and I almost blacked out.

It's pretty much all I've been able to think about. All I want is to be alone with her. I don't know if we'll have another chance like that before she leaves, though.

The Battle of Little Bighorn

So today in class I was just sitting there, trying to spin a little cocoon of warmth out of my body temperature despite the avalanche of chemical cold falling from the air vents in the ceiling, when Stipling humped into the room with two bulky plastic bags from Staples and an exaggerated version of her usual expression of grim purpose.

She put the bags down and withdrew a large, rolled-up laminated poster from under her desk. She tried to straighten it out against the chalkboard, but it kept like, jouncing back together. She'd get it pinned down and then reach for some tape, and then one side would roll up, which she'd smack down with her little hand, at which point the other side would roll up, and then she'd smack that down, too, and then try to reach for some tape again—she repeated this series of motions faster and faster until she looked like a berserk windup toy. Finally she cursed under her breath and made a quick motion like she was spitting on the ground and then let it slide down the board and onto the floor.

She turns around and starts taking things out of the plastic bags. There's a sort of anticipatory silence as she methodically arranges the materials—packets of index cards, pens, high-lighters, a stapler—on a desk.

She steps back and surveys everything, balls the plastic bags up and tosses them into the trash, claps her hands together, looks at us, and goes, "You all *know* the unit we're supposed to be working on is American history. It is now *time* to assign oral presentation topics." She raises her hand and goes, "Raise your hand, tell me what an oral presentation is."

Total quiet.

"*Hello.* Are you awake? Two words. *Oral. Presentation.* Anyone want to make a guess?"

A thick, woven silence.

The thing is, Roy Hassle never asked us actual questions. He mostly just steamrolled through the period with a series of non-sensical lectures he seemed to be getting from a huge binder with multicolored tabs in it.

Stipling is clutching a highlighter in her little knot of a fist. Today she is wearing a huge T-shirt with a smiling sun on it that looks like it was drawn by a six-year-old. She slams the highlighter down on a desk and claps her hands a few times and goes, "Hey! Wake up! It is now time to *interface!* Do you know

how to *interface?* If no one answers my question I will be forced
to call on one of you which I *will do!*"

Someone coughs.

"Fine," she says, picking up her clipboard. She scrolls down
what must be a list of our names. "Fine," she says more quietly
to herself.

I think she's going to call on me again but then she looks up
and yells, "Alvarez! Edward!...Edward Alvarez!"

"Eddie," says Eddie, sitting up in his chair.

"Mr. Alvarez," says Stipling, fixing on him, "would you please
go ahead and hazard a guess as to what an oral presentation is."

She's moved a little closer and I can now see that on her
T-shirt, under the smiling sun and on a cotton slope where her
breasts should be, it says, "Health Expo, Braddock County Convention Center, 2007."

"I mean," says Eddie, scratching the back of his head. "It's like
a presentation. You give it...and that's what it is."

"Very eloquent, Mr. Alvarez," says Stipling. She looks around.
"Would anyone else care to elaborate?"

Most of us are slumped down in our chairs. Eddie cracks his
knuckles and sits back.

"Well, Mr. Alvarez basically has the right idea," she says. She
straightens out her shirt. "An oral presentation is something you
give. It is a way to *convey* information to an audience, after which
they will hopefully have *learned* something about a topic. It is a
way for you to *organize* your thoughts around a specific subject,
during which you will highlight certain aspects..."

At this point my eyes are rolled into the back of my head and
there's a moat of drool pooling in the sides of my mouth. Then
I hear her say, "...in this instance, you will be working with a
partner."

She's like, "I have *secured* special research time in the

computer room. I have checked *out* books from the library. I have *provided* index cards and other materials for your use. Hey! Someone raise your hand, tell me what you might use an index card for."

She walks over to the desk where she put all the stuff from Staples and picks up some index cards. She shakes them in the air.

"Index cards! You use them to write things *down!* Notes for your presentation!"

I look around to see if anyone else is slightly unnerved by her shouting.

She puts them down and picks up her clipboard and says more quietly, "We'll talk more about the *structure* of your presentations later."

She starts going down the list and pairing us up with another person along with a topic. She was like, "Jamie Perkins and Eddie Alvarez, the Boston Tea Party. Aaron Wilson and Cedric Ames, the Constitutional Convention." And the more names she said, the more I knew who my partner was going to be. Finally when she was like, "Jacob Higgins and David Keffler, the Battle of Little Bighorn," I wasn't even a little surprised. I looked over at David for a second. He was smugly picking dirt out from under his fingernails.

"I expect you to work together. To divide responsibilities equally. You all *have* the ingredients. Now it is *time* to organize your thoughts."

I Have Never Written Anything Down on an Index Card and I Don't Mean to Make a Practice of It

When I think of the words *oral presentation*, it makes me feel bored and hassled like I'm standing in line on a hot day with a really messy sandwich and someone is asking me for directions. Which is why it totally motherfucking sucks that I now, because of a corn-on-the-cob-pin-wearing, flint-eyed, pointy-elbowed, flat-chested Janet Stipling, have to do just that. And with none other than the skiddingly grave and weird David Keffler.

I don't know David. I don't really like him. I only know these few facts about him: he went to Foxington Prep before he came here, his dad is on some planning committee, today was the first day we were supposed to work together.

So, great. I'm nodding off at my desk in classroom 107A while Stipling is talking some crap about the Gettysburg Address. Ten a.m. rolls around, which is when we're supposed to get together with our partner as mandated by the fifty handouts she's given us at this point. She's like, "Now is the *time* for you to get together and go over the *structure* of your oral presentation."

Everybody blankly looked in different directions. David's head was turned and he was staring at the door and I totally knew I would be the one to get up and go over there and that's exactly what happened. Finally people shuffled around and resettled with their partners. I pulled up a chair next to David's desk and was like, "Hey."

Stipling was apparently able to get the poster from the other day unrolled because it now hung down the blackboard and depicted a chaotic battle scene of soldiers in a smoky trench fighting other soldiers on bulging horses and said "Antietam, 1862." And that is what I stared at as David continued not to say anything to me. I also noticed for about the five hundredth time that day that I was freezing, and so I resorted to my heat-saving method of putting my hands in my armpits and rocking back and forth.

David was slumped down in his seat and staring into the distance like he was looking through a portal that no one else could see. I was like, "So…did you like, do any research?" He still didn't say anything.

I know that in terms of universal importance, this project isn't on the level of tracking down ex–war criminals who are now drinking neon-blue martinis next to a pool, or creating a shield that would prevent children from getting molested. But I also know that if I do a passable job it might get back to Lane and help me get out of here on time. And that if David never decides to say anything, it's going to be pretty hard to address such pertinent details as, Are we going to use index cards? Are we going to employ a chart? How much dubious information from the Internet are we going to cite? Will there be a book involved? At what point do we want to orient ourselves with this dumb battle in our nation's stupid history?

So finally, I get up and go to what is now labeled the "Project Materials" chair. Everyone is crowded around and in line to check out a pen, but I manage to find a packet of index cards. I go back and sit down and start unwrapping them. David looks over and makes this amused, air-slowly-coming-out-of-a-tire sound. He goes, "What do you want to do with *those?*" As if I'm the first person in the history of the world to consider using index cards in preparation for a presentation. I was like, "I don't know, *write* shit on them?" He goes, "Like what?" I ignore him.

Then I go stand in the finally shrinking line to check out a pen. But when I get back to the desk, I realize that it doesn't work. So then I go, yet again, to the project materials chair. By this time, the only thing left in the scratched-up bucket is a pencil with a little paper flag attached to it, which was kind of disappointing because the way I *pictured* working on this assignment was with a pen. I take the pencil and hold it up for Stipling to see. She's standing by the overhead projector and talking to

Eddie. She sees me and nods distractedly and I'm pretty sure she checks something off on her clipboard.

So back at the desk with David, I withdrew a green index card and sat there looking at it, trying to think of everything I knew about the Battle of Little Bighorn, which was nothing. There was the general white noise of people talking and shuffling paper, like some hum of efficiency and planning that only me and David were not contributing to. Also, Stipling was going around from desk to desk and I could hear her voice bobbing up and down and getting closer and closer.

Finally, I wrote, "The Battle of Little Bighorn." David snorts and says something under his breath. I go, "What?"

"Pencil is German."

I look at the little flag attached below the eraser. It had bands of gold, black, and red.

"I guess."

"Gestapo pencil."

Then I rewrite, "The Battle of Little Bighorn," because it seemed too faint the first time. The pencil slipped across the index card as if the lead was dipped in wax. I pushed harder. It was like trying to correct a swerving car. David said something else under his breath. Again I go, "What?"

"Pencil sucks."

"No shit."

"Great 'materials.'"

I go, "What did you expect? A marble pen and a crystal ball? This isn't Foxington."

"Yeah," he said. "Foxington. You've got me all figured out."

I stare at the index card. Under what I've already written, I decide to draw a dash, in the rare event that a fact should surface about the Battle of Little Bighorn.

David is sitting there, smiling smugly and flicking the inside of his palm. He leans forward and goes, "Do you want me to tell you something else about Josephine?"

I was about to ask who that was, but then I remembered him talking about her—his old English teacher. And then I realize something about David. Which is that he's one of those people who puts up a hostile front but really just wants to tell you all about themselves.

"Is this project about Josephine?"

"I went up to her desk once . . . ," he said.

I looked around. Stipling was hovering over two people, writing something in the air with a highlighter.

". . . to get a graded paper," he continued. "When she handed it to me, I saw that her fingernails were painted pink."

I could tell that David was expecting me to be really impressed with whatever outcome or punch line this story was going to have.

"And they had fake dewdrops on them."

"What?"

"Little, plastic bulbs on her fingernails, meant to be like, 'morning dew.'" He laughed a choppy little laugh. "She would want that. She would want everything to be *that way* . . . she wanted all of her moments to be like, under a waterfall."

I accidentally made eye contact with David, and to diffuse the expectant look on his face I said, "Weird."

"Yeah," he said, sitting back.

I looked back at the index card and started to feel the air going out of everything. It took a lot of effort to pick up my hand and write, "Part of the Civil War?" next to the dash.

"I mean, what was she trying to do? By asking to have her nails done like that," David was saying. I looked up. His voice was unshelled and normal-sounding.

"I just want to know why she got fake dewdrops put on her fingernails. I just want to know. And the frustrating thing is"— he pushed his hand through his hair—"I'll never know. Because if I asked her now, well, first of all, if she saw me, she would claw her eyes out and run away, but even if I did get to ask her, she wouldn't tell me, because *she* doesn't even know."

It was quiet for a while. Stipling was talking to some administrative person in the doorway, looking over her shoulder every few seconds. Everyone's conversation seemed to reach a collective pause. Someone yawned. And then the room became muddy with sound again.

I was rearranging some index cards on the desk in an attempt to look busy when David said, "She's like, really normal."

At first I thought he was still talking about Josephine, but then I realized, feeling kind of sick, he was probably talking about Andrea. I looked up. He had a cocky frat-boy sneer on his face, his eyes re-echoing with laughter.

"Who?" I said, gathering all the index cards into a pile.

"Your IHOP waitress girlfriend. C'mon," he said, affecting a wind-burned arrogance, "you can do better than that."

Usually when talking to people, you know what's being asked of you. You kind of get a sense of what's expected in the succeeding moments and have an idea of where the other person is coming from, how they're trying to maneuver and to what effect, and you can dispense whatever reaction you want to based on that information. But with David, right then, I had no idea how to react or how he expected the conversation to go.

I said, "You don't know anything about her."

"Yes I do," he said quickly. "I know her because I know that her brain is like a zoomed-in map. Thick lines and easy turns."

"Wrong," I said and started erasing what I'd written on the index card.

"I can tell, immediately, what people are like," said David. A little spit flew out of his mouth and landed on my desk. "When I first saw your girlfriend standing there in her normal way, I knew right then what she was like and I heard the sound of carpet being ripped out of the floor."

The eraser on the end of the pencil was hard and ancient and smeared everything around into a graphite cloud. So I tried to erase harder and created a sort of ragged, whirly hole. And that's pretty much what we had — an index card with a hole in it — when Stipling came around to our table.

She holds her clipboard to her chest and goes, "Uh-*huh*." She's like, "Well. I can see you're really col*la*borating." Then she goes, "All right. Where's your outline worksheet?"

Neither of us said anything. I was staring at the poster again, of the soldiers in the trench.

She goes, "I would like you to reach back into the farthest depths of your memories to yesterday, when I handed you an outline *work*sheet, which you were supposed to use today."

We were quiet again. She stood there for a few seconds, tapping her pen on her clipboard. Then she blasted us with a battery of questions:

"Where is your worksheet?"

(Don't know.)

"Have you done any research?"

(No?)

"What have you been doing in the computer room if you haven't been researching?"

(Expanding my online poker protectorate.)

"Are you aware that this project is being graded and will factor into your evaluations?"

(I am now.)

It continued like that for a while. She made her signature

gesture of pretending to spit on the ground and kick an imaginary pail with her little foot. She started to move to the next group, but before she did that, she turned around and looked at me.

"Mr. Higgins, did you have a question?"

I'm like, "No," and then she turns around and walks away.

Later, at the end of class, we all turn in our pens. I turned in the one that didn't work, the one I got initially. And I thought, at the time, that David turned in the pencil. But now that I think about it, I didn't actually *see* him do it.

Social

Last night I found myself in the cafeteria again, at the first social we've had since they'd been postponed because of Jamie Perkins's disruption of the last one. When I heard about it, I was pretty psyched because considering the socials are, in fact, mandatory, it was a guarantee that Andrea would be there. We haven't seen each other since movie night. She's leaving next week, which I've been trying not to think about. But yesterday morning, when I allowed the thought to float up, I realized that it could be the last time we'd get to hang out.

I got there first and immediately positioned myself next to the snack table. There was the usual selection of chips and cookies left over from snack time, with the new addition of a bowl of transparent, really hard-looking different-colored candies. I picked up a purple one, thinking it would be some interpretation of the flavor grape, and stuck it in my mouth. I must have been nervous because then I drank, in pretty quick succession, three cups of soda and ate another candy, all of which made me feel super-jittery and like my hair kept getting in my face.

I also registered a middling stream of classic rock coming

from somewhere. I turned to see a little stereo set up on a plastic chair. Other new touches included a dish of glitter on the games table probably meant to be employed in some craft setup that never came to fruition, and napkins that said "Volunteer Appreciation Weekend 2007!" on them. Other than that it was the same kind of thing, with everyone standing around listlessly drinking soda, not socializing.

The girls started filing in. I didn't see Andrea and was struck by this sudden bolt of fear that maybe she'd gone already and I'd been confused about the date. But finally she was there. She was the last one. She looked around the cafeteria and when she located me she walked straight up to the games table, which is where I was now standing.

She said, "Hey," and so did I. I was really relieved. Just hearing her voice made me feel better. But then, for some reason, I couldn't think of anything to say. She licked her lips and looked at me expectantly and was rocking back and forth on her feet. I looked down. And then around the cafeteria. It was pretty quiet. There were some voice scraps coming from whatever paltry conversations were taking place. The music stream had dried up into a rock bed of static.

I looked at Andrea's hand and thought of the last movie night, when it seemed like her palm was a warm room that I had entered where I wanted to lick the walls. I wanted to go back there. I looked back up at her face. "How are...I thought maybe you had left already" was my opener. But I think I said it too casually, like maybe I didn't care that she might have left, because she seemed a little taken aback.

"Oh, no," she said. "Next week. Tuesday." She put her hand up and held one of her eyelids closed and shifted her weight to one leg.

"Cool," I said. And then I said something that in my most

fucked-up dreams I never thought I would hear myself say, which was, "Do you want to help me put together this huge puzzle of Mount St. Helens?"

We both looked down at the games table. The puzzle was in a wide, frayed cardboard box that depicted the volcano in almost neon brightness.

Andrea was like, "Um...I guess?"

So we took it over to a different table and pulled up some chairs. A few people looked at us with curiosity, because I think it was literally the first time anybody had actually used one of the games. And that was confirmed after we opened the box and spread everything out and realized that like half of the pieces were still stuck together.

We took them all apart and spread them out. Deciding to convert my anxiety into some sort of forced enthusiasm about the puzzle, I clap my hands together like an idiot and go, "Okay. We should probably start with the sky."

Andrea was like, "Really? Because all those pieces are the same. I mean, don't you think we should start with the ones where something is like, *happening?* Like the pieces that have both sky and volcano in them?"

I was like, "Oh, yeah. Duh."

So we did that for a while. We still weren't really talking. I watched her fingers forage over the table. I ate another one of the hard candies I'd brought over from the snack table. I actually *gulped,* like a cartoon character or like people do in movies when they're nervous. It sounded like a sound effect.

I was about to say something. I was about to be like, "Are you just going to go back to Staunton?" when suddenly Jamie Perkins and Denise Henly were standing right there.

Denise was like, "You guys are putting together a puzzle," in a singsong voice. Jamie started making these swirly motions with his hands over the table. He goes, "What if I just fucking like, fucked this shit *up*?" Denise started laughing. I was like, "That would be shitty?" Then Denise changed her tone and was like, "This girl is fucking awesome," referring to Andrea. "What you said in class today—fucking awesome." Andrea was looking down. There were those clouds of red wandering across her face.

None of us said anything. Finally Jamie was like, "Let's go mess with Officer O'Connell," and they walked away.

We sat there staring at the puzzle. We had managed to put together a band of evergreens. I said, "What did you say in class today?" Andrea slowly looked up. Her eyes fixed on my face. She goes, "Are you bleeding?"

I go, "What? No."

She tilted her head to one side. "Yes you are."

"No," I said, "I'm not."

She leaned over, extended her arm, and softly touched my lip. I suddenly felt like sap running down a warm tree. There was so much I wanted to tell her. So much I wanted her to understand.

She sat back and held her hand up. There was blood on her fingers.

"Yes," she said, "you are."

I had cut myself on an air bubble in one of the hard candies. I could feel the wound on my lip with my tongue, a tiny little metal-tasting flap.

She got up suddenly and said, "Here, I'll get you a napkin." I sat there, completely still. I didn't want to move. Not even a little bit.

When she got back, there was a sill of wetness on the bottom of her eyes. She started talking really fast. "I think I'm going to go back to Staunton for a little while and live with my aunt. I want to visit Alaska, where my brother lives? Have you ever been there? I was thinking, I could save up and go see him. Maybe when you get out of here, you can come, too." She had balled up the napkin in her hands.

"Yeah," I said. "Yes."

We had been avoiding each other's eyes all night, but now we stared at each other. I was in a corridor, floating in space. Guilt-free, absolved. She's the prettiest girl I've ever seen.

The lights clicked on. I looked down at the puzzle. We had just begun the volcano.

Computer Room III

Today was Internet-research day for our oral presentation projects. We got extra time in the computer room and were supposed to work with our partners. I don't like working with David Keffler and wish I could just do this thing myself, but I figured this would be our one chance to fatten up our outline, which, considering that neither me nor David has taken advantage of the books that Stipling checked out from the library or done any research on our own, contains nothing.

When we started walking to the computer room, I thought I was pretty prepared because I had managed to withdraw the balled-up outline worksheet from the paper graveyard under my bed. Not only that, but I had smoothed it out and even managed to keep it with me all day so I'd have it for the computer room. I also found the index card we had used in our last meeting, the one with the hole in it, and in an uncharacteristic streak of ambition decided to go ahead and take that along, too.

We get there and it becomes clear that Mrs. Dandridge has actually assigned computers to us. And in accordance with whatever system of petty triumphs she uses to buoy her stupid life, she stuck me and David with the most obviously sucky one: computer number four, whose keyboard is covered with a plastic sheath and which is next to an overbearing spiky plant. Bitch.

David is in front of me in line, so he gets to the computer first and takes the chair that is farther away from the plant. So when I get there, I have to awkwardly sit under it, with its plasticky leaves poking me in the back of the neck. I might as well also mention that the poster in the computer room has been changed, yet again. The new one says "Laughter" in a swoopy font. It has a picture of two little girls falling into a sand castle.

There's nothing like a poster that says "Laughter" to remind you what a shitty mood you're in. And how a sterile, too-cold computer room isn't exactly the bouncy unmade bed of humor. And how nothing has had even the slightest aura of funniness since Andrea left.

Mrs. Dandridge is like, "Everybody! Everybody!" waving her clipboard around. She's like, "I'm sure you know that you have an hour in the computer room today. I expect you to use your time wisely. And out of respect for your classmates, I trust that you will keep your voices down."

David has his arms crossed and is slumped in his seat. I take it upon myself to log on to the computer. Neither of us says anything as it takes five hundred years to load the JDC homepage. David said something under his breath that I didn't hear. I go, "What?" He's like, "Google." I'm like, "Yeah, thanks."

This is when I kicked into my usual self of not wanting to do anything. Each one of my fingers felt like separate migrant workers in the hot sun as I typed "The Battle of Little Bighorn" into the search field. Not to mention the fact that it took me about five tries because of the plastic sheath.

Research Park

Let me just say that researching the Battle of Little Bighorn with David Keffler was not exactly a stealthy navigation of the facts leading to exciting and uncouth conclusions. It was not exactly a glinting research park with square shrubs and everyone walking around purposefully. And what is the point of doing research when you know you'll never find out exactly how something *was?*

You can cull information, tally all the facts, log the necessary details, and make some assessments, but that's only coming from your personal plaza of logic. It doesn't mean that something was really the way you think it was. It's like with Andrea. I thought about her, researched her, collected all the facts. I could make an outline about what we said and did, but that doesn't mean I know what happened between us. You can't quantify what it was like when I first saw her, or how it feels now that she's gone, or what it was like when her hand was inching up my leg in the rec room that night.

You can't reduce and dismantle how it felt when she shoved her address into my hand in the courtyard yesterday. She ignored me the whole time. And because I thought she was ignoring me, I ignored her. What does research ever uncover? Only conclusions that you wanted to find.

I was over by the broken water fountain. It was seeping from the bottom, creating a puddle on the cracked concrete around it. When I saw Andrea come out through the door, I expected her to come right over to me. But she didn't. She stood talking to Denise against the opposite wall. Half her body was in the sunlight, the other half was in the shade.

May 11 was the day I saw her for the first time. It was in the cold cafeteria, under fluorescent lights, the last place you would think something would actually happen.

June 8 was when we first talked to each other. It felt momentous at the time. Like a day that should be memorialized, planted with an obelisk. But the only way I can understand the importance of any event is based on my interpretation of how things are *now*.

June 23 was the day we talked about sneaking into the Blue-Star Pavilion together once we were both out of here.

June 30 was the day she almost gave me a hand job in the rec room. Was that day a victory? What is the importance of an almost–hand job? It felt, at the time, like the puncturing of a new future. But maybe it was just another almost–hand job in a long pointless chain of almost–hand jobs. I mean, the only historical significance anything has is the amount you assign it yourself, based on what you want to believe about the way things turned out.

I don't know how things turned out. I don't know what happened. It's like something that I've been carrying around in a hidden pocket this whole time, and recently I've tried to take it out and unfold it. I've stared at all the creases and studied the fibers. I've squinted at it and turned it around in all different ways. I've closed my eyes for a long time and then opened them quickly, like the sudden, blunt configuration would offer a picture I would instinctually understand.

July 9 was yesterday, my last chance to see her before she would leave today.

She's standing by the wall, talking to Denise. I felt weird going over there so I pretended to watch the basketball game happening between Eddie and Desean and a few other guys. Eddie threw me the basketball and as I caught it, I glanced over at Andrea. She was looking at me and Denise was gone. I should have thrown the ball back. But for whatever reason, I caught it and joined the game. I could feel her eyes on me the whole time.

It was almost time to go inside. I was really sweaty. The game dispersed and we started to make our way back toward the entrance to the building. Andrea was still against the wall, bobbing up and down on her feet. I felt sick and couldn't look at her face, because now it seemed so obvious that we just should have talked and why did I choose to play basketball? I got closer and closer and finally I looked up at her. She reached forward and took my hand and shoved this folded-up piece of paper into my palm. "It's my address and phone number," she said.

Everybody wallows in their own set of vague conclusions formed by whatever information is at hand. Jim will never know who shot JFK. Pastor Todd will continue to sit back in his La-Z-Boy of religion. Lane will keep smugly relying on her Eastern calendar sayings as if that passes for therapy. Everyone will continue to shade themselves in the little burrow of supposed meaning they've gouged out for themselves while the world spreads out around them in rolling hills of nonsense. But no one will know anything. You've got to look at a big map to see exactly where you are. Therefore no one will ever know anything because it's impossible to ever know everything.

But I did find out that Andrea lives at 1349 Grove Street in Staunton, Virginia. And I also know that when I unfolded the piece of paper and saw her handwriting, which is disheveled and full of thin, casual loops, I thought I was going to throw up.

Back to the Computer Room

Some shit about General Custer comes up. I just sat there. I thought about writing it down but I didn't *feel* like it. But that's what other people were doing. I looked around, and Eddie Alvarez was even pointing to the computer screen with his pen like he was on the cover of some business pamphlet. The thing is, I'm not really used to writing down facts in service of a project. I yawned and stretched back. Then I sat forward and in my mind I was like, "Okay. Let's do this."

I was about to write "General Custer" on the index card when I realized, yet again, that I didn't have anything to write with. That was a setback. You would think that when you actually decide to do something that's legal and requires effort, life would cut you some slack. David was staring off into the distance. Every once in a while he would laugh a little under his breath.

I finally got up and walked to Dandridge's desk. She was reading a paperback called *End of the Line*. I took one of the many pens out of the tin on her desk and started walking back to my desk. She goes, "*Mister* Higgins." I stop and turn around. Her mottled hands were folded on top of her book and she was staring at me like an engorged suburban cat that wants to attack but is too lazy to get up.

I go, "*Missus* Dandridge."

She's like, "When you take something off someone's desk, it is considered polite to ask them first."

In my head I was like, "Suck a dick, suck a dick, suck a dick." But I look down at the pen and say, "This?"

"Yes."

"Oh, you were using it?"

"No. I was not using it, but that doesn't matter. It was on my desk."

There were people watching at this point. I stood there. I wanted to tell her to fuck off. I wanted to tell her that her smug look of expectancy put her in line with Nazi lieutenants and racist prison guards and anyone else in history who has ever asserted their arbitrary authority for no other reason than to make someone feel inferior.

But I knew that at this point I had to pick my battles. And if I said anything, Mrs. Dandridge would be more than happy to report to Lane that I'd been acting up in the computer room. So I somehow managed to wrangle my voice into saying, "Can I use this pen?" and she said, "Yes. You may," with the kind of satisfaction that ripped through me like shrapnel.

When I got back to the computer I was totally exhausted. David was in the middle of doing some origami shit with our outline worksheet. I sat there with the pen in my hand and the plant poking into my neck. I had lost all motivation to write down anything about General Custer. I finally clicked on Mine-sweeper and figured I'd just do that for a while.

Research hour ticked along. I was so wrapped up in my game that I didn't even notice Mrs. Dandridge going around and checking on everyone until she was basically upon us. I looked down and saw that David had made a series of paper birds and barely had time to minimize my game before Dandridge was looming over us like the moon eclipsing the sun.

She was looking at me with the same satisfaction in her eyes that she'd had when she made me ask for a pen. She folded her hands and said to us both, "I assume you've been using your research time productively?" We were silent. David crushed one of the paper birds in his hand. "May I ask what it is you're researching today?"

"The Battle of Little Bighorn," I said.

"Excuse me?"

"Little *Bighorn*."

"Fine," she said, straightening out her sweater. "And what have you found out this hour, since I *know* you've been working so very hard?"

I went blank. I was about to make something up, when David started talking. We both looked at him. His eyes were locked on Dandridge and he was speaking in a low, instructive, singsong voice.

"Also known as Custer's Last Stand, the Battle of Little Bighorn found American soldiers outnumbered by Cheyenne and Sioux Indians on the Rosebud River in Montana during the summer of 1876. General Custer's men were annihilated within an hour. Most of the bodies were skinned and mutilated because the Indians believed that would prevent them from entering heaven."

Mrs. Dandridge was squinting at David and massaging one of her hands. She started to say something but David interrupted.

"General Custer's body, however, was skinned but not mutilated. Some believe this was because he wasn't wearing a uniform and therefore the Indians didn't think he was a soldier. Others believe it was out of respect for his reputation as a great leader."

Mrs. Dandridge sucked in her breath, and David goes, "It's widely believed to be the worst American military disaster ever."

We were all still for a second. Then Dandridge goes, "Good. Fine," and waddled away.

That's pretty much the most I've ever heard David talk. It was crazy to hear him actually string sentences together.

I was like, "So you've been researching?"

"No," he said. He was trying to smooth out the paper bird. "We learned about all this shit in eighth grade at Foxington."

"Oh," I said. "Well, that was pretty awesome. Dandridge was like pointing a rifle at us and you took it and bent it into a hat like at a kids' party."

David sort of smirked and goes, "I guess."

I looked at the paper birds he had made. They were lined up in front of his keyboard.

"What are those?"

"I don't know," he said. "What do they look like?"

"I mean, where did you learn how to do that?"

He hesitated. He picked one up, the smallest one, and looked at it really closely. "I just learned it," he said.

David Breakdown

Having been forced to spend a significant amount of time with David Keffler, I've started to break down the component parts of what was previously a pretty inscrutable personality. It took me a while. And it wasn't a task I was necessarily psyched about. But when you have to collaborate with someone on a report about the battle of motherfucking Little Bighorn you can't help but notice a few things about them.

David Keffler is in possession of a huge amount of undirected rage. Unlike Pastor Todd, who has converted his emotions into unsettling monologues about Jesus Christ, or me, who sublimates my anger with sarcasm, David has yet to find a way to manage it other than through scalding bouts of silence and a just generally creepy vibe of really simmering about something. In the revolving settings of high schools I attended and then got kicked out of before coming here, I've met other people like David, because people like him seem to take a liking to me.

They're all really smart, and really sullen, and have over-attentive yet clueless moms you always kind of feel sorry for. They mostly come from stable backgrounds. They gestated in the light of like five hundred finished basements. They think everyone is stupid.

David is from Canterbury Park, which is a gated housing community next to Reston Town Center. There is a little booth at the front where you have to show an ID card in order to get in.

Inside, the houses are really big and close together with sculpted shrubs out front and every once in a while a strange rock formation. In every front yard there is a little sign with a lightning bolt signifying a really intense security system. It's very quiet and no one is ever outside.

The only reason I've been to Canterbury Park is because a girl I dated once, Sarah Tipply, was from there. Her parents were jazz-loving zombies and had three different kinds of pepper.

Anyway, sometimes I have these blinding flashes of psychic intuition about people. Today I was watching David methodically fill in a corner of a piece of paper with pencil so that it was black and shiny and curling upward, when I suddenly could just *see* him sitting quietly in a renovated basement, nestled in the couch cushion palm of Canterbury Park. The only sounds are the faint trumpets of the news his parents are watching upstairs. He's gorged on the claustrophobic convenience of sliding glass doors and pillows of descending sizes. And now he's just sitting, planning a specific kind of revenge.

It's like there was some malfunction in the valves and chutes of Canterbury Park. Something went wrong in the carpet-lined fetus. And when the sculpted shrubs opened and produced a person, it wasn't the doctor, lawyer, or future owner of an intense security system. It was David Keffler.

He hates everything. He hates index cards. He hates General Custer. He hates having to sharpen a pencil. He has a series of contemptuous air-pressurized sounds he'll make with his mouth whenever anyone says anything. He's very still. He doesn't have many gestures that would indicate the subconscious management of being bored, or thinking back on something funny someone said, or waiting for something. He never like, shifts his weight or taps his knee. The only thing he does in that category is flick the inside of his palm with his other hand.

And when he's annoyed (which is always) or when someone like Mrs. Dandridge or Stipling is approaching, he'll start doing it faster. His hatred seems clinical and divvied out equally among everyone here.

Which brings me to the point of this journal entry. Which is that I think he might be planning to do something.

Through this project we've managed to form, if not exactly a friendship, a kind of grudging acceptance of each other. Ever since he bulldozed Dandridge in the computer room, we've stopped being actively hostile toward each other. The other day he even got me an extra index card from the project materials chair.

And he's become more talkative. By talkative I mean he's become more cavalier about sharing his bitter assessments of everyone. Mrs. Stipling is a "flat-chested slut," Mrs. Dandridge is a "transvestite walrus," Pastor Todd is simply a "homo."

We were in class the other day, supposed to be working on our presentation. I was drawing a decrepit cityscape on an index card. David goes, "Hey," all furtively as if I was one aisle over in a library and not right in front of him. I was like, "Yeah?"

He points toward the ceiling with his pencil. "You ever noticed how the smoke detector in the rec room always beeps?"

"Yeah."

"Yeah, well it stopped beeping."

I thought about it for a second. "I guess so."

"Means it doesn't work."

"Or someone changed the battery."

"No," he said. His mouth contorted into a wet smile. "They didn't. It happens all the time. Someone takes the battery out to stop the beeping and then forgets to replace it. The smoke detector in the rec room—you can see that it's been turned but not fixed back in the right position. And it doesn't have the red light that flashes every forty-five seconds like the others do. That thing is completely dead."

"Fascinating." I went back to drawing my cityscape.

"You know what else?"

"Huh?" This was the longest conversation we'd ever had. I was getting kind of uncomfortable because he was staring at me so hard. Usually when I look at him there's something sealed in his eyes. But now whatever it was had opened like a lolling freezer door.

"The fire exit? The one in the rec room that's supposed to lead out to the west exit of the building? It's blocked. By the TV and DVD player and all those cords. You ever notice that?"

"No."

"Well, I did. Do you know what *that* means?"

I shrugged my shoulders.

And now I had the distinct feeling that he was testing me, moving along cautiously with his words, mining for a certain reaction.

"It means if there was a fire, the only way to get out would be through the front entrance. You'd have to go down the main hallway past the cafeteria and everything. Might take a while."

I could feel him waiting for me to say something. When I finally looked up, he was staring at me like he had just very carefully stacked something up on the table, like a tower of wineglasses, and he was impishly waiting for me to be impressed.

"Are you like, really disappointed in the JDC for violating fire codes or something?"

He looked down, disappointed. "You know what I'm saying," he said quietly. And we didn't talk for the rest of the hour.

Condor Court IV

In the house on Condor Court, there was a picture in the hallway above the stairs of a majestic hawk swooping down through
a canyon washed in pink light from the sun. It was a pencil
drawing made of lots of little feathery strokes. The artist's signature was scribbled in the bottom corner. I remember staring at it.
I don't remember when it was, if it was before or after we found
the coke, or if it was one of our first days there. I just remember
standing there and staring at it.

One afternoon Rocky and I were on our way down the stairs
when we heard the front door open. We both froze. We looked
at each other. Whoever it was, if they had turned to the right and
walked a few steps, they would have seen us. But they didn't. It
was one person, and he turned to the left and walked toward
the kitchen.

My heart felt like a buffalo stampede. I looked around and
everything was unfamiliar, like I'd never been there before.
Me and Rocky crept back up the stairs. It was easy to be quiet
because of the carpet. We peeked over the landing that looked
down at the living room and were about to start back toward the
master bedroom when a man walked by below us. He looked
Mexican. He was wearing jeans and a baseball cap and a blue
flannel shirt.

Rocky started moving away. He mouthed to me, *"C'mon."* But
I couldn't move. "He'll *see* you." But I was caught there, snagged,
and any struggle to get away would make him see me. I knew
that he was going to walk to the fireplace, move the little brass
fence aside...

When he saw that what he was looking for wasn't there, he started
cursing in Spanish. First with disbelief, like if he had stubbed his

toe really bad. And then with anger. And then with regret. His voice got bendy with remorse. Then he stopped altogether and just stood there, looking into the fireplace. He took off his hat and wiped his forehead with it. He studied his thumb. He put his hands in his pocket. He stood for the longest time, just staring.

Eventually, right when I felt like I couldn't stand it anymore, like my body was going to explode to rebel against being so still, he backed away, turned around, and left.

Snack Time

Okay, David Keffler is fucking crazy. That is a fact. I guess I'd always suspected it, but today in the rec room during snack time it became jarringly and unpleasantly clear.

I was sitting at one of the round tables (the sofa was taken), having procured a number of especially stale strawberry wafers. I had decided to take them apart in order to make a master strawberry wafer by putting two icing sides together. I was in the middle of my little surgery, with everything laid out in front of me on the table, when David Keffler sits down and is like, "What are you doing?"

I was like, "What does it look like I'm doing?"

"Leveraging your underutilized assets," he said, sitting back.

"What?"

"Nothing. That's how my dad talks."

"Oh." And then I remembered hearing that his dad was on a bunch of committees. "Sounds like a dick."

"Yeah."

I had taken the tops off three wafers and now had three bare icing sides. I was trying to decide whether to scrape the icing off one and graft it onto another, or to just place all three together, effectively making a triple-decker.

"Have you thought at all about what I said the other day?"

I decided to play dumb. "What? The other day when?"

He sat back again and was quiet for a while. I decided to forgo the triple-decker idea and just put as much icing as I could in-between two wafers. I was making kind of a mess. Also, I had handled the wafers so much that they were getting brown from the grease on my fingers, which was grossing me out.

"Have you ever seen live piranhas?" said David.

"Nope."

"My dad has a tank of them in the lobby of one of his offices. He thought it would be funny."

"Weird."

"Everything," David said, flicking a crumb off the table, "in my dad's office is coordinated. Everything. From the colors in the paintings on the walls to the special tissue-box holders to the carpet. Everything is from the same like, muted color palette. I bet he would even make his receptionist, *Allison,* wear those colors if he could. I guess it projects like, a certain cohesive business image."

Aaron walked by. He goes, "Jake, man, are you *trying* to make a mess?" and then left before I had a chance to respond. I looked down and there was a deserted battlefield of strawberry wafer carnage on the table: broken parts and smears of icing, crumbs everywhere.

"I usually had to wait around in the lobby. Allison would always offer me a tissue. But most of the time I watched the piranhas. You could see their teeth. And there were gold coins at the bottom, like for decoration."

David continued: "I wanted one of those gold coins. But I didn't think of trying to reach for one until after I'd watched the tank for a while. There were about five or six piranhas, swimming back and forth. So you'd think it would never be safe to stick my hand in. But if you watched for long enough, there was a gap every once in a while. A small amount of time when the piranhas were all at the ends of the tank and the water was clear. It wasn't very much time. But it was enough."

I decided to eat my master wafer. It was warm and too sweet and when I bit down on it all the icing came out of the sides.

"Blind spots. You have enough of them strung together and you've got an open field. It's like this place. They think they've got us all locked up in here, that it's fail-safe, totally secure. But there are times when no one's watching, there are things that no one notices. But I notice. I notice when certain things fall into place and a gap is created. One that's so wide, you could stick your hand in. They think it's so secure, but there are times when this place practically bends over and waits for you to—"

"*Damn it,*" I interrupted. I had gotten a crumb in my eye and was trying to paw it out. "What are you *talking* about?" I also felt sick from the chemical sweetness.

"I'm *talking* about lunchtime."

"I still don't know what you're talking about."

He was flicking his palm. "Think about it. At lunchtime, the receptionist woman, Jan..."

"It's Joan."

"No, it's Jan."

"No," I said. "It's Joan."

"Well, then, who the fuck is Jan?"

"Jan is someone else."

"Fine, whatever. *Joan* sits outside on the bench in front, eating her fucking panini or whatever with that jumble of keys on her belt. She wouldn't be able to hear what was going on...that's one exit. The other exit, in the rec room, is blocked. Those are the closest to the cafeteria, the ones they'd try to herd us to first. The other one is way the fuck down the hall by the computer

room, but by then, with the smoke coming through the vents...
I mean, if there's one thing about this place, it's well ventilated.
Smoke would tear through this building, these vents and air
ducts, and by that time, this place would be a fucking zoo."

"You want to set this building on fire."

"Um, yeah, I think that's obvious."

We fell silent. I realized that I had crushed what was left of my
master wafer in my hand. There were colonies of crumbs on my
sweatpants. My fingers were sticky. It seemed unnaturally quiet.
I looked around quickly but everyone was at the same regular
tempo of sitting, being restless. No one was paying attention to
us. Aaron was crunching plastic snack trays into a bag. David
was looking at me expectantly.

"Why?"

"Why what?"

"I mean... *why?*"

He looked down and then traced a circle on the table. Then
he looked back up at me. "Okay," he said. "Maybe I've misjudged
you."

"Whatever," I say, getting annoyed. "Good. Because it's not
like I'm standing in line to hear your bitter, fake high-school-
shooter philosophy."

I didn't expect him to burst out laughing but he did. He
heaved soundlessly back and forth. I also managed to cull some
sort of sweat-crumb paste on my palms and I was trying to wipe
them off on my sweatpants.

"You know what I hate," he said, suddenly serious. I didn't
answer.

"More than anything? Those seashells on Stipling's vest. You
ever notice that? She has actual seashells sewn onto her vest."

David stopped talking for a minute, and then seemed to
refocus.

"The reason I picked you—"

"You didn't pick me," I interrupted.

"What?"

"I mean you didn't pick me. The only reason we're sitting together right now is because of the oral presentation we were *assigned* to work on together. You didn't pick me for anything. We're not like, in this together."

He sat back and a liquid smile spread across his face. "Okay," he said, "just tell me when you want to know what the plan is."

Choices II

Two things happened today. The first is that I got a letter from Andrea. I was lying on my bed during free time, shading in some levitating orbs on the sketch pad Jim got me (which I'm finally allowed to have—"Just make sure you use these in a responsible way, okay, Jacob? Can you do that for me?") when Aaron comes in and holds out a big manila envelope. I looked at the letter and looked up at him and said, "What's that?"

He goes, "It's a letter."

I look back at the letter. "It looks like it's from Russia."

"Just take it."

Then I recognized the handwriting on the front. I took the envelope, waited for Aaron to leave, and then opened it. This is what it said:

Dear Jake,

I'm back! (In Staunton). My stepmom rearranged my room. She put a picture of a tiny baby with flower petals around its head on the wall. It has a coffee stain on the side.

How are you?

Something weird happened to me yesterday. There's an overturned bathtub in our backyard and I was sitting on it. Then I noticed a green snake curled up at the bottom. I thought if I got off the tub it would bite me. So I sat there forever. Now I'm sunburned.

How's the food in the cafeteria? Does it still "defy classification?" haha.

Well, gotta go.

Andrea

p.s. Sorry about the big envelope.

I read it over and over again. I turned it over, turned it back, smoothed it out on my pillow and then read it some more. It was written on a piece of torn-out spiral notebook paper. It had seams like it had been folded and unfolded a few times. I looked in the manila envelope again to see if there was anything else. There wasn't.

I didn't know how to think about it. For the past few days I've been picturing Andrea how she was in the courtyard, with smudged light on her cheeks and a strand of hair accidentally getting into her mouth and how she would absentmindedly start to chew on it and I could almost see her insides. But this letter and that memory don't go together.

So that's what was going on, that's why I was more annoyed than I even would have been when the second thing happened, which is that Pastor Todd came to visit again. I was feeling disoriented and like I needed to think more when he knocked.

I looked up to see him smiling, his face as wide open as a board game. He goes, "Hey Jake! Neat drawing." Even though I'm pretty sure he couldn't see my sketch pad from where he was standing.

I go, "Oh, hey," and then looked down again at the letter,

hoping that, despite what I knew in my heart (that he was going to try and convince me to come back to his office for another "meeting"), he would just move on.

Pastor Todd goes, "I just remembered that we were supposed to have another meeting today."

I go, "We were?"

"Well, *yeah*."

I'm like, "Is there any way...because...didn't we kind of cover it the other time?"

Pastor Todd doesn't say anything. He leans back and erupts into his unnerving and misplaced laughter. He straightens himself out and says, "Right on," and continues to stand there, one foot in my room, one foot out. And that's when I realized that he wasn't going to leave without me. I felt, not for the first time, his almost hostile insistence; his complete inability to register signs of resistance no matter how reasonable. And I knew that he would continue to pave over any hesitation on my part with blank cheerfulness.

So I figured I would go, because that would require less energy than trying to make him leave. I figured I could just sit there like I did last time and tune him out and then it would be over and maybe he would get the picture and give up. I figured it would be easy and I wouldn't have to invest anything. But that's not how it happened.

Even though I went with Pastor Todd, I could feel this aluminum anger start to throb in my teeth.

We get to his office and I slump down in the chair. He sits down at his desk across from me. There was a fat pen on top of some papers. Half of it was see-through and had a tiny ship in it. It read "Hello, Seattle!" Pastor Todd caught me looking at it and goes, "Isn't it wild?" He picked it up and tipped it and we both watched the ship float slowly downstream. "Best city in America."

He put the pen down and smiled at me. "We missed you at Bible study last week."

I stared at the pen.

"Oh man, on Tuesday we had a great discussion. See, that's the thing. It's more of a *discussion* than a study session," he said, making these motions with his hands like he was trying to sculpt a ball of clay.

"We cover it *all*."

Someone must have stopped by the doorway behind me because Pastor Todd appeared to be kind of hassled for a second. He looked up and pointed to his wrist like where a watch would be. Then he did that grownup kind of flingy hand gesturing that would indicate a later rendezvous. I turned around but I didn't see anyone. He goes, "Oh, that's just Jan.

"But anyway, Jake, I think the reason that our Bible study sessions are so successful is because people feel like they can say whatever they want." He leans back. "This is not your Mom's Bible study." And then he looked kind of impressed with himself and I had a feeling that he'd been planning to say that for a while.

The phone on his desk rang. Whenever something interrupts Pastor Todd's flow, the relaxed veneer that clings to him like a wet receipt dissolves and for a second you can see the grim determination underneath. He picked up the phone with barely concealed irritation and said, "Hello? Can you just make it say something else? Well, you can buy them at . . . you can buy them at . . . right. The stick-ons. If you buy the stick-ons, you won't have to staple them. That'll be fine. And just make it . . . hello?"

He puts down the phone and kind of straightens himself out.

And then he started talking in this way that made me feel like he'd jumped the script a little in order to get to the main part.

"God's plan," he said. "On Tuesday we talked about God's plan. How God has a plan for everyone. We went around and discussed what it was for each of us. Jamie Perkins said that he thought that God's plan for him was to work at Jimmy's Tire Center once he left here. Denise Henly said she thought God's plan was for her to make up with her stepdad and take some computer classes. We went around and the whole group said something. What I want to know is, what do you think God's plan is for you?"

There was a silence as I debated whether or not to respond. Pastor Todd leaned back and made a steeple with his hands. Then we started talking at the same time. I said, "You mean...," and he said, "I just..." He sat forward and said, "Go ahead."

"You mean like, what job am I going to get once I leave the center?

"Well, yes. I mean, what do you think God's *plan* is?"

"You mean, what do I want to do?"

"Well...sure." He sat back.

I didn't say anything. I was getting so sick of his lame circling. I kept staring at the pen. I shifted in my seat like I do in Lane's office when extreme inward annoyance compels me to recompose my body.

He continued: "The beautiful thing is, once you leave this juvenile detention center, you get to choose your path. You get to—"

And then I interrupted. I go, "What?" I think we were both surprised to hear me talk again.

Pastor Todd stops talking, blinks, and says, "What?"

I go, "What you just said."

"What I just said?"

"It doesn't make any sense."

"What doesn't make any sense?"

"You just said you get to choose."

"You *do* get to choose." And then he kicked into gear and started talking as if he had said what he was saying a million times before. Like he had memorized the most effective inflection for each word. "God granted man free will so that he may choose to walk in the light, so that he may deny depravity and pick the righteous path toward heaven."

"Yeah, but that doesn't make sense with what you were saying before."

"About what?"

"About God having a plan."

"He does have a plan. He has a plan for everyone."

"Yeah, I *know*, that's what you keep saying. But I mean, can the plan be wrong?"

Pastor Todd burst out laughing. He picked up the Seattle pen, leaned back, and tapped it against his cheek. "I don't think so. Brotherman is all-knowing." He pointed the pen at the ceiling.

Most people in the course of an argument or discussion can kind of sense it when they've misstepped, crossed some logical boundary. This is not the case with Pastor Todd.

"Yeah, but that doesn't make any *sense*."

"I'm not sure I follow you, Jake."

"What I'm saying is, how can you *decide* if God already has a plan? I mean like, Denise isn't choosing to take some computer classes if God already knew she was going to."

Pastor Todd looked at me and then his eyes moved slowly to the left of me and into the distance. He started to say something and he stopped. Then he said, "It's like when you know someone really well. Like they're your best friend and—" He abruptly stopped talking again. "Okay," he said, leaning forward. "Say you've got a kid in front of you and you're offering him two things. In one hand you've got a rotten apple and in the other hand you've got a pair of really neat sunglasses. You *know* he's going to pick the sunglasses."

"I mean," I said, "that's still just a prediction."

"Well"—he quickly scratched at something behind his ear with the pen—"there's no *way* he would pick the rotten apple."

"Yeah but there's no way you would really know that," I said.

"Oh, I know it," he laughed and looked around for confirmation as if from a studio audience. "Have you ever met a kid?"

"Yeah but you don't *know* it know it."

"Well..."

"I mean," I continued, "people do things all the time that you didn't think they were going to do."

"Yes."

"Even someone who you know really well could do something you didn't expect."

"Correct."

"So...what the fuck?"

Pastor Todd is smiling and biting his lips and looking into the distance. He shifts in his seat.

He abruptly leans back and puts his hands up. "Speaking of sunglasses," he says. "Did you know that the people in Seattle buy more sunglasses than in any other city in the nation?"

Without waiting for me to answer, he slams his fist down on a stack of papers on his desk and goes, *"What!"*

He recomposes himself. "Neat. Stuff.

"Well, cool!" he says. He pushes down a button on his phone and looks at the time on the digital display and says, "Gotta go ahead and cut this session short. Let's get you back to your drawings."

We have another silent walk back to my room.

In Which I Go to a Random House, Eat with Strangers, Am Reincarnated

As I've mentioned before, this place functions on a system of crappy awards that are supposed to reinforce positive behavior. Toward the end of your sentence, if you've managed not to knife anyone, you're allowed out of the center for some sort of unspecified outing with your sponsor. So last night I was invited or, more aptly, required, to go to dinner at Jim's house with his pregnant wife, Amy.

There I was, standing on the concrete steps in front of the center, with Officer O'Connell idling nearby, my first taste of freedom in almost six months. As I waited for old Jim to come sailing down the river in his Honda Civic, I looked around, wondering, I guess, if things might be different from how they were when I first got here. But it was all blaring with sameness—the top of the Staples behind the overpass in the distance, the boring pine trees, the barbecue restaurant on the corner.

Then, passing through all the neighborhoods to get to Jim's, Whitlow's Quarry, Cedar Mountain, The Ponds (there is no pond, quarry, or mountain in any of these neighborhoods), I was confronted with the same monotony of strip malls and trees that compose Braddock County and I realized that it is probably always going to be the same until it gets blasted away in a nuclear war.

Turns out Jim lives in a duplex next to the Greenpond Shopping Center, which actually isn't that far from where I live, or used to live, with my mom. I had a friend who worked at a Greek restaurant there, so it was weird being in that area again with this random guy.

We go inside and I meet Amy, who I hadn't really been that curious about, but who looked pretty much like I would have pictured, except more pregnant. Her stomach stuck out so far you could have stacked some paperbacks on it. It made me kind of uncomfortable but didn't seem to bother her. She was pretty nice, though, and clean-seeming, and had freakishly small fingernails and pink hands.

This baby, whoever it's going to be, has hit the parental jackpot, though, because Jim and Amy could not be more prepared. Whenever they say her name (it's going to be a girl and they're going to name it June which I didn't ask they just kept telling me about it like I give a crap), their eyes look up as if they're seeing a hot-air balloon in the distance and they kind of have to snap out of it. This was all part of the dinner conversation, though. Before that we sat in silence watching TV—the news and then some low-budget sci-fi show. I kept on looking at a picture on top of the television of Jim and Amy dressed up like farmers from when they visited Colonial Williamsburg.

The oven beeped and then Amy hefts herself forward and goes, "Well, guys," with her eyes and cheeks bobbing up and down. Jim helped her up and we went to the kitchen, which was like one foot away, and then we ate. There was a skinny vase of flowers on the table, surrounded by a plastic string of fake leaves which I could tell they had probably put there for me because it looked absurd and out of place, and so that was embarrassing. Dinner was chicken surrounded by vegetables. It tasted clean but not in a bad way. And to drink we had carbonated apple juice.

I had predicted that dinner was going to be really awkward, and I can't say I was too far off the mark. Jim started talking about a comment he had left on a conspiracy blog, when Amy snapped her head up and looked at Jim in a way that caused him to take a left turn into an anecdote about losing a laundry list. Amy talked about running into her old ice-skating teacher.

I continued having an inward epileptic seizure from being so bored. I was about to excuse myself to go to the bathroom but was really going to ransack the upstairs for anything pharmaceutical, and might have been the first person to overdose on contact lens solution if I hadn't suddenly found myself engaged by the pregnant female stranger sitting across from me, Jim having left the table to get the phone.

I go, "What?" and she goes, "Oh... I just asked how the food was, at the center." And I go, "Um... it's not that good." And then for some reason I go, "Thanks." And then she goes, "You're... welcome." And then I looked at her for a millisecond and her skin was very smooth and then I flashed to Beans's grizzled face and suddenly felt brushed by a sadness that seemed to come from the center of the universe.

So yeah. Dinner was a real carousel of uncomfortable emotions. Things picked up a little when Amy brought out a plate of little cookies for dessert. They looked boring but then turned out to be a taste rodeo of strawberry and chocolate, and which I ate about all of them.

Jim's brother died in a car accident when he was my age, on some winding road next to the place where they grew up. How do I know this? Because Jim told me after dinner. I thought we were going to go back to the center, but then the two of us went out onto the back porch so Jim could smoke a cigarette. I know, it's totally weird. Who knew that Jim smokes? He goes, "Since I was fifteen. Could never fully shake it." And then offers me one. Which I take and it felt good, but not that good because I was never much of a smoker.

So we're standing out there, both hunched inward because there was a chilly breeze, and Jim said that cold weather always reminded him of his brother, who when he was a kid tried to run away one winter, and they found him in a pay phone booth with near hypothermia five miles outside of town. I asked why his brother tried to run away and Jim said that he didn't really know.

Then I didn't say anything and Jim was kicking the porch with his shoe like he was trying to remove some gum, and he looks up at the sky and then back down and launches into this thing about how his brother was supposed to be in a mental institution, but his family couldn't afford it and also no one really understood Ely anyway. And then one day he ran his car into a tree close to their house. He stopped talking as fast as he had started and it was quiet out there. Over the fence and in the distance I could see the light coming from the mega-store parking lot.

The realization came to me that Jim thinks I'm his reincarnated little brother and it wouldn't take a prize-winning psychiatrist to figure that out. I guess I could have gotten angry or felt weird about the whole thing, but I didn't. I just understood it.

Maybe it was all the fake alcoholic apple juice but I suddenly had this unfamiliar impulse to consult Jim about something. To talk. I couldn't figure out how to form what I wanted to say, though. Jim dropped his cigarette and then stubbed it out with his shoe and then bent down to pick it up. Finally I was like, "You know how you were saying before…about the conspiracy?"

His eyes lit up. "Yeah! Well, which one?"

"Oh yeah, there's tons of them." I felt like I should have been able to cite something he had said before in order to open up the way for more conversation, but I still wasn't sure what I wanted to say. I kept going, though. There was a surge in my brain to staple something down.

"But like, about Oswald," I said.

"Yeah, yeah," said Jim. I could tell that he sensed that I was trying to get at something and I wasn't sure how to do it so he tried to make the field fertile by dropping all these seeds. He was like, "Yeah, Oswald, Jim Garrison, and then...Bay of Pigs and—"

"No. Yeah, I mean. But, yeah, but so, you think that Oswald had like, people that knew what he was going to do?"

"Well," said Jim, "I think it would be ignorant to assume that Oswald acted alone. That he didn't tell anybody. The thing is, all it takes is two people to qualify as a conspiracy. Just two people. That means that even if Oswald told only *one other person,* the Warren Commission is—"

"Yeah so, but like, he probably told someone else. So...I mean, what do you think that person did?"

"Did?" Jim lit another cigarette. He offered me one but I declined.

"Yeah, I mean if someone tells you something like that, are you supposed to like, do something about it?"

I looked down. I didn't want to make eye contact because I felt like we were already in new territory of earnestness. We were operating on a level where there was actually a hint of a larger concept at play, something verging on personal. I mean, at least for me.

I could feel Jim choosing his words strategically. "I guess it would depend," he said, "on whose side you were on. But if there was the possibility that innocent *people* would get—"

"Yeah," I interrupted. "Yeah I mean what if..." And then I couldn't finish.

We stood in silence for a while. I kept on feeling a match scraping in the back of my throat to say something, but I didn't. Finally Jim was like, "Well, I better get you back to the center."

We drove back the way we had come, through the neighborhoods with all their houses lit up from the inside. We pulled up in front of the center where Aaron was waiting. Jim sucked in his breath like he was about to say something, but then he just turned to me and said, "Well, good-bye, Jacob." I was like, "Later." Sucks about his brother, though.

My Mom Is in the Hospital

Beans, Erin, my mom, is in the fucking hospital. Refrigerator Man put her there. He might have killed her this time.

They brought Jim in to tell me and I knew, just by looking at his face, that something really bad had happened. His expression wasn't one of embarrassment, or anxiety at having to bear bad news. It was disappointment, like something had finally challenged his outlying optimism.

I was in class. Stipling was in the process of awkwardly hoisting up a textbook in order to offer us a pan-view of a picture inside when Officer O'Connell came in and whispered something to her. She goes, "Huh?" and he tried again. Then she looked at me and nodded to him. When we walked out everyone stared at us wondering what I had done or what had happened to me.

I saw Jim before he saw me. He was sitting in the cafeteria and had his paper clip out. Something he was thinking caused him to quickly shake his head like he was trying to get water out of his ear.

When we entered he stood up so fast his chair shot out behind him. It seemed like he was considering giving me a hug, then decided against it. He said, "Hey, Jake," and motioned for me to sit down. I felt like I was in the center of a bull's-eye. It's like I heard the strains of an old song I couldn't remember until finally it came to me, the inevitable chorus, "Your mom is hurt! Your mom is hurt!"

But that's not what Jim said. He was talking in slow motion. I watched his mouth contort into all kinds of weird word shapes until he finally formed the one he'd come to say:

"Coma."

"What?"

"Erin is in a coma."

"What do you mean?"

He started talking but I interrupted and said, "I know what a coma is, but I mean, what the fuck? Is she going to *wake up?*"

He wouldn't tell me exactly what happened. He was playing with his paper clip. He barely looked me in the eye. But it doesn't matter. Because even though I don't have the exact details I can still see it. I might not know the specific contours of this situation but I know the DNA. It's always the same.

Erin would have been coming home from her cooking class. She would be driving our old Ford Escort with the screwy axle. She would have her huge tote bag with her. She'd probably be tired as she turned off the car and undid her seatbelt, trying not to touch the scorching buckles because she always hated how hot they'd get in the summer. Then she'd get out of the car and Refrigerator Man would be there.

If he hadn't been there, she would have gone inside and heated up a microwave dinner. Or watched TV. Or marked something down on a calendar and stared into the distance. Or folded some clean towels. Or just sat quietly, not drinking, with the kind of stretched stillness she seems to be in possession of lately.

But Refrigerator Man *was* there. Probably pacing on the front porch. Or no—he's too lazy to pace. He would have been sitting on the concrete step, squinting into the sky, yawning, annoyed at the sun for being hot. Annoyed at the sky for carrying the sun. Annoyed at the concrete step for being hard; annoyed at anything for even presuming to exist, especially in the face of his bulk, his square footage, his massive dominion of blame.

I've asked myself before how he got like that—what scalding life injustice from his past made him this way? But there's no point in asking. Like certain natural deposits in the earth, Refrigerator Man just is. And he always has been.

Maybe it would occur to Erin to tell him to leave. That she had a court order. Maybe she did tell him to leave, at first. But I have no doubt in my mind, none at all, that she eventually invited him in. She would have seen in him whatever it was that always made her take him back. Some bandwidth of light visible only to her. He would have smiled his slow, lazy smile.

Then they'd be in the kitchen. Erin would sit him down at the table, get a beer from the fridge, and crack it open for him. Or no, he would have brought beer, knowing that she wasn't supposed to have any. He'd get the same twelve-pack he always got from the convenience store down the street. And he'd open one for himself, leaving the dusty case on the table to tempt her while she leaned over, exposing the spotted, overly tan basin of her chest to place a microwave dinner in front of him. He'd nudge them toward her and say something like, "Remember that time on the carousel?" or "For old time's sake. It's me, Steve."

And I don't know what happened. If she eventually took one or not. But I know she would have laughed. Smiled like she does for him, with her whole face, like she's turning it to a fresh breeze. She'd put her hair up and take it down, put it up again. She'd tell a story with exaggerated gestures. She'd touch her collarbone. For a while they'd sit there and bask in each other. And anyone watching would think that they were just two people.

But then it would turn. Maybe he got annoyed because she wasn't drinking. Maybe he got annoyed because she was drinking too much. Maybe it was because she asked him to leave. Maybe it was because she asked him to stay. It could be anything.

You can never tell with him. Sometimes he would beat on her for letting the ashes on the end of her cigarette get too long.

But it would turn and she'd be able to tell because you can tell if you're used to it. It's an almost imperceptible change. A subtle downshift.

Her smile would erode. He'd slam his fist down on the table and say, "Damn it, Beans, why can't you let me be myself?" or "What are you trying to insinuate?" And then he would rage on her. Come over her like a storm cloud made of skin, suddenly possessing a stealthy kind of energy where all the damage in the world can be siphoned into a few well-placed blows. There would be these sounds: a few sickening thuds, the sudden release of air, the paper-towel rack being ripped off the wall.

And then it's over and she's on the floor, unconscious, or sprawled over the kitchen table, and Refrigerator Man sits back down and cracks open another beer after a job well done. A hard day's work. Physical energy exerted to optimal effect. He smiles to himself in his little beer-induced moment. A wasp pings against the screen window. A little fireworks display goes off in his head that says, "Don't Fuck with Me" in falling sparkles. Weak moms of America, your soft skin and helpful bending elbows, don't fuck with Refrigerator Man.

I never wanted to hear my mom make that sound. The sound of sustaining a blow. The sound of the paper-towel rack being ripped off the wall.

He'd continue to sit there in quiet. Eventually he'd say, "You gonna get up?" and he'd look around. "You, uh...you gonna get up?"

She's at Thomas Jefferson Hospital on Rio Road in intensive care with a coma that could lead to brain damage, a broken collarbone, and a punctured motherfucking lung.

I Don't Know What to Do

With this anger. It's like walking in a screaming neon forest where leaves keep getting in my face. It's like having some hidden gill open in my side that breathes only the pure, alpine air of hate.

I don't know what to do with my hands. It's hard to write this. I feel perched and super-aware, like a lizard. Or anything else with the instinctual, ancient knowledge of the dumb rhythms of the world. Of course this was going to happen. Of course this pattern was going to continue. How could I ever have thought that I had snagged some afternoon riff of regular being?

The past few days it's like I've been living on the Sea of Sympathetic Eyes. After Jim told me what happened and I got leave from class I sat on the edge of my bed and stared at the wall above the grunt of a sink in my room. Jim sat next to me and put his paper clip away, and we were like that for a long time.

Aaron came in a few hours later. I was in the same place. He sat on the sink in front of me. "I heard about your mom," he said. He rubbed the back of his neck. "My family...I mean, there was some stuff, too. My parents just couldn't..." He put his fingertips together as if to indicate a structure. Then he put them by his side again. "It doesn't matter. I'm just saying that your mom is going to pull through, you know?" He sat there for a while and then said, "I know this shit isn't fair."

Pastor Todd came by later that day. He peevishly looked into the window. We made eye contact and he disappeared. A few moments later he came back, all contrived gravity. He gave the two-knock indication that he was going to push the door open. He stood there with a shiny paperback in his hand. I was on my stomach, drawing a series of circles on my pad. I looked up at him, and then back down. I squeezed my pencil and pressed down so hard on the paper that the lead broke. Inexplicably, thankfully, he turned around and left.

I haven't said a thing to anyone since I found out that Erin was in the hospital. My silence is as hard and stuck as a park bench in the winter.

Lane

"Jacob, I just want to say"—I'm in Lane's office, staring past her to the books on the bookshelf—"that I've heard about your mother and I'm very, very sorry."

There's something different about Lane today. When I got to her office she wasn't playing Solitaire on her computer like a zombie. Her face didn't go through its usual course of expressions—mild surprise to resignation—upon seeing me. She was sitting in her chair across from where I'm supposed to sit, with my folder in her lap.

Also: her voice was different. It was tentative and there were particles in it that I haven't heard before.

She exchanged a knowing glance with Officer O'Connell and then looked at me and gestured toward the sofa. She watched as I walked toward it and sat down. I didn't pick up the denim pillow.

I stared at a book called *The Dance of Anger*. There was another one called *Codependent No More*. There was one that faced out on the bookshelf. On the cover was a watercolor picture of a teenage girl staring out the window.

If there was ever a time when I might have actually engaged with Lane, that time was over. I feel like the dead letter in a flickering sign.

"Do you want to talk?" She stopped abruptly and looked down. Then she engaged in this series of gestures that would lead a person to think she was uncomfortable—crossing and recrossing her hands, sighing loudly, biting her lips and looking out the window—and I wasn't sure if they were genuine or not. But I decided not to waste any of the little energy I have left on caring.

"We haven't always seen eye to eye," she said. A few papers were sliding out of the folder on her lap and were about to fall to the floor. When she finally noticed, she slammed her palm down to stop them. She straightened them out and blew some hair out of her face.

"I've been distracted, I think. I know I haven't said anything about this, but my sister has been sick. And so I might not have...I think it's been difficult for us to talk to each other."

You know how you'll be watching TV or a movie or something, and there'll be this scene of a blackout, where you'll see some city at night from the top, these pastures of sparkling light which will, section by section, go completely dark?

"When you first got here, you were so very angry. And it seemed like, after time, you started to...well, when you first got here, it was like you were a"—she held her fist in the air, squeezing her hand—"tightly woven *baseball*."

I looked to my left at the calendar picture on the wall—a close-up of two sand dollars on a wet beach. I can't believe I almost subscribed to that shit. That I was almost at a place where that calendar was okay.

Lane relaxed her fist, and for a moment her fingers separated and wavered in the air. "But after a while," she said, "it seemed like you started to unravel...no, that's not the right word." She pinched her lip.

I can't believe I almost bought into everything that calendar symbolizes with its swoopy font, its lame attempt at playfulness, its language of domestic peace; the country-time bullshit assumption that the world is okay, filled with peaceful linen moments.

"I don't mean un*ravel*," said Lane. "I just mean that after a while, it seemed like you started to, oh, I don't know"—she shifted in her seat—"loosen up?" She was surveying my face for some reaction, some recognition.

I almost got in line with everyone else to buy that calendar at some cosmic normal-person bazaar. I almost didn't mind looking at those sand dollars.

"It would just be such a shame if this one incident with your mother could cause you to...forget all of the progress we've made."

Just Tell Me When You Want to Know What the Plan Is

It's to douse the sofas in the rec room with carpet cleaner found in the cleaning cabinet, which, according to David, is highly flammable, during chore time. This shouldn't be too much of a problem considering Aaron's "supervision" of cleaning hour amounts to doing a crossword at the snack table and rhythmically smacking a pen against his chin.

David will then position one of the trash cans, in which he's made a large mound of crumpled paper, next to the sofa and under the arm that juts out a little.

The critical moment will occur after we've filed out of the rec room and are on our way to the computer room, when David will raise his hand and tell Aaron that he forgot his outline worksheet and needs to go get it. Aaron will either tell David it's too bad, or he'll let him go, in which case, David will set the trash can on fire with a book of matches from the Barbecue Tavern that he stole from his dad during Family Day.

The trash can will set fire to the sofa which will set fire to the burlap curtains in front of the whiteboard which will set fire to the ceiling, which will *not* set off the smoke detector. At this point we will all be in the computer room, pounding on the space bars.

"There's no way...," I said. We were sitting in class. I was pretending to highlight relevant passages in a printout. Stipling was hovering over a different group at the other end of the room. "...that's going to work."

David was pretending to organize some index cards, shuffling and then reshuffling them. He spread them out on the table, gathered them up into a neat little pile, put them down, and looked up.

"Because?"

"Because the only way something like that would work is if we lived in a completely different world, where like, things were slightly easier and clicked together more and everything turned out like you thought it would."

He respread the index cards out in front of him, as if he were showing his hand.

"People make plans. Plans work. Even here. But out of curiosity—"

"For starters," I interrupted, "I mean, just as one thing out of many, how do you know that Aaron would really let you go back?"

Eddie, who was sitting over at the next table with Keith, theatrically crumpled a piece of paper and threw it over his shoulder. We both looked over for a second.

"I did a trial run about a month ago," said David, talking in a lower voice. "We were on our way to the computer room and I asked Aaron if I could go back to use the bathroom. He was pissed but then he was like, 'Make it quick.' Plus, I'm not a

troublemaker. There's no reason for anyone to pay special attention to me."

I thought of the victim awareness session when he made that
face. Lane was there, she saw it. And Aaron was there, too.

"I don't think," David said, "that you have a firm grasp on how
not hard it is to start a fire when you have a match and a bunch
of flammable shit around."

I capped and uncapped my highlighter. He shifted forward
in his chair.

He continued: "Okay. One of my dad's projects is this office
park in Herndon. Do you know how much shit they have to
do to fireproof new buildings? Frame fireproofing, building par-
titioning, automatic fire suppression systems, pressurized and
fireproofed exit stairs. Not to mention like, just having a basic
sprinkler system. This place doesn't even have that. This place
has a bunch of blocked exits, a smoke detector that doesn't work
in one of its biggest rooms, and some slut eating a panini outside
the locked door at noon every day."

I suddenly had the feeling our pantomiming was really transparent and if anyone were to look at us it would be obvious we
weren't doing any work. I searched the room for Stipling. She
was standing over by her desk, jerkily folding up a tissue that
she then shoved into her pocket.

"Still," I said, "the fact that you've got something worked out
in your head doesn't mean something won't mess it up in real
life. You've got this recipe, this like, long division problem..."

David laughed. "Divide with gasoline," he said. "Multiply with
flames. Subtract happiness and being. Bring down fiery ceiling
panels. Remainder: maximum elongated mouths, burning hair,
general major discomfort. Exploding denim couch."

I looked down at my highlighter. It's a stupid plan. I know it is. I know it's not going to work. I could see David kind of gluttonously turning it over in his head. I decided to go to the front of the room and get one of the many random books that Stipling had checked out for our use. I took one off the top of the stack. It had a picture of a canon sitting in what looked like a dewy morning battlefield.

"That could be any war," said David when I sat back down.

"What about us?" I said.

"What *about* us?"

"I mean, in this airtight plan of yours, to burn down this building, how would we get out?"

He looked up at me.

"Well, you know what exit isn't obstructed. You can go directly there before the smoke or fire gets everyone else."

He switched two cards around.

"So you're going to—"

"It'll be easy," he interrupted, "to get away. If that's what you want."

Stipling walks up to our table, surprising us both. "Well, I can see you two can actually *talk*," she says. "Might prove beneficial seeing as this is an *oral* presentation." She lowers her clipboard a little. "I'm looking especially forward to your presentation because Little Bighorn happens to be one of my favorite topics." Neither of us says anything.

She says, "Sittin' Bull."

More quiet.

"Well, whatever," she says. "Keep it up." The seashells on her vest rattle as she walks away.

"Can't you just see it?" says David. "Lane's denim couch, erupting into flames." He molds an explosion in the air with his hands. "*Whooooosh.*"

"So let me get this straight." I cap and uncap my highlighter. "I mean, what exactly do you *want?*"

He picked up the book and started paging through it.

He started saying something, then stopped. Then he said, "What I want, is a world calculator. Because you think things don't happen, but they do happen. For instance, I want to know how many women slip and fall in the shower each year. Do you ever think of that? They slip and fall and probably rip down the shower curtain. If I was a composer, I'd line them up and have them all fall at the same time. Can you hear it? A national tide of shower curtains being ripped down, all at once." He closed the book and put it back on the desk. "I'm going to do this. It is within my capability."

"What if I stopped you?"

"Yeah, right."

"I could say something. To anyone. I could say something right now."

"Why would you?"

"Why wouldn't I?"

"Well, if you did," he said, "it would just prove my theory."

"Which is?"

"That everyone's a dead end. Besides"—now his face was locked up—"you can't stop me, because this was always going to happen. Everything is in the process of disappearing, and this place was always going to burn down in a fire. You think you can stop it? *You* think *you* can stop it? You can't. The only thing you can do is be a part of it. I thought you would understand that."

"What did you do?"

"What?" This whole time he'd been looking at something over my shoulder. Now he looked at me.

"What did you do? To get in here. Why are you here?"

He sat back and started playing a pretend violin.

"I stabbed someone in the hand. Logan Shiflett. This guy in my English class at Foxington, *Josephine's* class. He's one of these guys—bulky Adam's apple previewing some big man bullshit. He was always leaning over me to talk to Ally Glick like I wasn't there. And every time, he put his hand in the exact same place on my desk. So, one day, I brought a carpet knife to school. There were lots of them around the house. In class, at my desk, I pushed the blade out as far as it would go. Then, when he did what he always did, when he put his hand on my desk to lean over me and talk to Ally Glick, I stabbed him. Between his thumb and pointer finger."

David breathed in and smiled placidly like the air was nourishing him.

"I haven't thought of that in a while."

A Cabinet Full of Plates

I've been lying awake a lot. It never gets completely dark. When we go to bed they don't turn out all the lights. You would think you would maintain a mariner's sense of time in here, where you could tell the hour by some internal metronome without having to see any natural light. But the ability leaves you, and at the appointed moment, 9:30 p.m., they ladle dimness onto your day like a side portion.

I've been thinking about swimming, about what would happen if someone dumped me into a pool or lake where the water was too deep to stand. If, at the last minute, I'd be able to do it—the world leveling, proportion and equilibrium meeting up in a kiss of balance, instinct kicking in like I'd always known how. My arms and legs would synchronize, my body would glide by, doing backstrokes, reveling in the freedom of knowing *how to be.*

These past few days, I've been going through the motions. Trying not to think too hard, filling my head with the sand of routine. I don't make eye contact. I don't talk to anyone. The little piles of food on my tray in the cafeteria resemble shoddy graves and I haven't been hungry. I jostle my limbs to perform the necessary functions. In the morning, my eyelids are like two rusty garage doors.

Lately, Stipling has been looking at me with an expression I can't decipher, and today she took me aside after class.

We were supposed to be filling in a worksheet. I was sitting with my head on the cold desk when the quickening of sounds around me indicated that it was time to go. I looked up to see her staring at me.

She was looking through some pages in a binder, and as I walk by she goes, "Mr. Higgins, I'd like to speak to you."

I stand there as the rest of the class files out. Her mouth is scrunched up to the side as she flips through the pages with small, violent flicks of her wrist.

A week ago, this would have annoyed me. As I was standing there, I would have had to figure out how to negotiate restlessness with the right amount of feigned interest. I would have wondered, with irritation, what was going to be asked of me in the succeeding moments. But now I had the dominion of an inanimate object. I was a gift card with nothing written on the inside.

We're like that for a while, her flipping through the binder with that air of grown-up distraction and me just standing there, when she finally slams it closed and puts it on her desk. She turns to me. She's wearing a boxy floral jacket-type thing over a white T-shirt tucked into blue jeans. This is the closest I've ever been to her and I can now tell that she smells like a combination of baby powder and pet store.

"I heard about your troubles," she says. She puts her hands in her front pockets and rocks back and forth on her feet.

"Now, I'm about to tell you something. It's of a personal nature and might not be appropriate, but I *don't* really care."

She takes her hands out of her pockets and hooks her thumbs into her belt loops.

"While back," she says, "when I was still living in Marfa..." She changes pace a little. "Now I know you spent some time in Texas, and we don't have to get into all that, but what I'm saying is that you probably remember how flat it was."

I don't say anything.

"Well, that's where my family is from and I was living out there for a while. It came to be that I was living with my husband outside Marfa. Now I'm not someone who cares a whole lot about *stuff*"—and with that she makes quotes in the air with her fingers—"but I did have one thing that I cared about."

As she was talking I noticed that she had a skin-colored plastic cuff attached to her ear that seemed to be connected to some sort of hearing apparatus inside.

"It was a cabinet with plates and teacups and saucers in it. My grandmother was a painter, and she painted all kinds of dinner plates with little scenes...Christmas and farms and whatnot. And she gave them all to me before she died, and I put them in this cabinet."

Stipling checked her watch. She straightens out her jacket and takes a step closer to me.

"Now my husband and I, at that time, were having a lot of trouble. It was right before we separated. We had been fighting all day. And I *do* take responsibility for some of the way things were."

Her eyes were fixed on me and I felt frozen in the canal of her quickly moving words and it was then that I realized what a hard little rivet of a person she was. I pictured her floating in space, struggling to hold two panels together.

"We had been fighting, and I was upstairs in our room feeling pretty low. I knew we were going to split up. I had medical bills and I felt nauseated all the time. I was just sitting there..."

I pictured her perched on the edge of a bed covered with a homemade quilt in a room battered with cleanliness.

"...when I heard a crash outside the house. I'll tell you something," she said. "I knew what it was even before I went to look. I knew it in my heart. And then when I went outside it was confirmed. My husband had rolled that cabinet out the front door, down the driveway, and into the street, where it fell over and everything—not a plate survived—broke."

I didn't know where to rest my eyes. They finally settled on the overhead projector in the corner of the room behind Stipling.

"Now, keep in mind this was during my sickness. I was in the middle of chemotherapy. I didn't have anybody, my grandmother's plates were broken, and I was real sick."

She said, "Listen to me."

I looked at her.

"I'm not telling you this so that you feel sorry for me. I'm telling you this so that you know something."

She straightened out her jacket again.

"Which is that things don't *get* any easier."

Wake Up. Eat. Walk.

Lift hands. Lift feet. Sit there. Compose body. Recompose body. Feel eyes in sockets. Crack knuckles. Realize there is no point in cracking knuckles. Wet lips. Cough. Yawn. Configure facial features into neutral expression. Put face on autopilot. Allow things to pass through body. Listen to unidentifiable electrical hum coming from somewhere. Drag pencil across a page. Tug at eyelashes. Breathe. Continue to breathe. Empty out a trash can. Wipe down a window. Walk across various rooms for various reasons. Offer necessary responses. Place hands on a keyboard. Avoid heavy eye-contact lanes. Try to keep warm. Look at hands. Bite skin beside fingernails. Get bored of doing that pretty quick. Drag toothbrush across teeth. Turn on faucet. Plug sink. Let water well and rise and keep rising until it starts to overflow. Turn off faucet. Stare at lake. Realize that there is always an unidentifiable hum coming from somewhere. Lie down. Look at ceiling. Put hands on chest. Put hands on balls. Put hands to the side. Close eyes.

The Day After Tomorrow

Yesterday when I passed David in the hallway, he mouths the words, *"One, five,"* as in fifteen, as in the fifteenth of August, which is the day after tomorrow, which is when he's supposed to start the fire.

I've been thinking that maybe he wasn't serious. The last time we had to work together on our oral presentation in class, he didn't say anything about the fire. But then today he happened to be in the courtyard at the same time as me.

It was overcast and windy out there. The concrete was drying from what must have been a recent downpour. Every time someone bounced a basketball, a little spray of drops would bloom around it. I was sitting on one of the red steel benches, staring at my feet, vaguely registering the scattered sounds around me, trying to keep warm and waiting to go back inside, when I sensed someone standing in front of me. I look up and it's David. He's holding a basketball and he's more pale than usual in the clammy, filtered light of the overcast courtyard.

"You wanna play?" he says, holding the ball at his chest.

"Uh," I say, confused, "do *you* want to play?"

"What?" He bounces the ball, it makes a wet sound, he catches it. "You don't think I know how? You think I spent my whole life playing videogames and like, mixing household chemicals?"

"I don't really know." I knock my sneakers together.

"I have been known," says David, spinning the ball in his hands, "to physically exert myself."

At first he seemed challenging, like he wanted to fight. Then he seemed game and joking. Now he was staring at me with what I thought was curiosity.

"Hey," he said, and he rocketed the ball at my chest with an amount of force I didn't think he was capable of. I caught it, but it almost made me fall back off the bench.

"Jesus." I straightened myself out. "What the fuck is your problem?"

"I just want to know if you're ready for tomorrow." He was looking at me with that marble arrogance again. He leisurely picked something off his shirt and flicked it into the distance.

"You're full of shit." I threw the ball back at him and stood up. I wiped my hands on my pants and looked around. It didn't seem like anyone was paying attention but then I saw Aaron over by the door, eyeing us, his head cocked like a deer sensing something in the woods.

"You don't think I'm going to do it." David dribbled the ball once. It must have hit a stone or something because it bounced to the side and he had to lurch to catch it. He lost some of his composure and looked at me furtively.

"You think I'm like, not serious?" He threw the ball at me.

"No. I kinda don't." I threw it back.

"You're wrong," he said, smiling to himself, lovingly tracing the seam of the ball with his forefinger.

"It's not going to work," I said. I should have walked away. I don't know why I didn't. I looked over at Aaron, who was now talking to Jake.

"What?" said David. "You think things don't *burn?*"

"I know things burn," I said.

"You just wish you'd thought of it."

"Oh, yeah," I said. "Every day I'm like, 'Wow, I really wish I could think of bullshit ways to burn down municipal buildings.'" I kept on wiping my hands on my sweatpants, even though there was nothing on them.

"I mean," I continued, "even if Aaron does let you go back to the rec room, and even if you do manage to set the trash can on fire, someone would walk by and notice and put it out with a fire extinguisher or like, a cup of *water.* And even if that doesn't happen, there are other smoke detectors in this building."

"You can tell everybody that," he said, still studying the ball, smiling to himself, "when they're ping-ponging around these walls, trying to figure out which way to run."

It had gotten darker out there. A gust of wind flattened our shirts against our chests.

I go, "Whatever," and was about to walk away when David threw the ball at my chest again. This time I dodged it and we both watched as it bounced over wet concrete toward the brick wall.

"Denise Henly," he said.

I hesitated. "What about her?"

"You know her, right?"

"Sort of."

"You probably never noticed this, but she has a tattoo on the back of her neck. A small martini glass. It's kind of blurry, like she got some inbred second cousin to do it with a baby pin." David laughed petulantly, impressed with himself.

"So what?"

"I just wonder what it would be like," he said, suddenly serious, "to be melting and to be Denise. To be a melting Denise Henly. 'No!'" he yelled, imitating someone burning. He pulled his cheeks down with his fingertips, elongating his eyes. He burst out laughing.

"You know what hair smells like when it burns?" he continued. "Bad. It smells really, really bad. I bet Lane's hair will be the first thing to catch on her body. She'll be in like, a headlock of flames." David looked into the distance, squinting his eyes. "I wonder what if feels like when your eyelashes are on fire."

"No one is going to burn."

"Don't get *mad*," he said. "You just don't want to admit you're enjoying this. You're enjoying the fact that you'll know where to go while everyone else is running around. You're enjoying being on your little porch swing of knowledge. Don't pretend like you're not. Don't pretend that you don't want all of this to happen."

"Why do you think you know what I want?" I said.

"It's like your mom's boyfriend," he continued, his features set into an expression of faint amusement. "And her recent stint in the hospital. Like *that* wasn't going to happen."

"Fuck you." I stepped forward, toward him. He crumpled backward but didn't stop talking.

"It's simple—"

"Shut up," I said. "Stop talking."

"What? You don't think that one thing follows the other? Have you ever seen someone throw a rock into a lake? I mean, what do you think is so unlikely about me wanting to do something and then doing it? About enacting a series of motions I've been thinking about for a long time?"

He began counting off on his fingers. "Lane, Pastor Todd, fucking Janet *Stipling*. You know what? All those little beads and seashells are going to pop off her stupid vest and she'll be like, 'I had a double mastectomy, blah, blah, blah.' Maybe she'll try to lecture the fire into leaving her alone, but she won't be able to because nothing can save her."

I looked around. People were starting to disperse, walking toward the door to go back inside.

"But even if the fire doesn't work," said David, "I still have Germany."

I stood there, hesitating. He stepped closer and squinted his eyes.

"Think."

"The pencil," I said.

He smiled.

"It's just a pencil," I said. "Are you going to try and erase someone?"

"In a sense," he said. "The point is that when presented with the right like, nook of vulnerability, and when you know how to use it, anything can be a weapon."

He was staring past me as if envisioning how everything would unfold.

I looked around. It felt like it was going to start raining again. Most everyone was huddling against the walls. I walked away.

Refrigerator Man Is Out on Bail

I found out this afternoon. Officer O'Connell came to my room to tell me that Jim was here to see me and my first thought was, "My mom is dead."

I've become like an archaeologist of Jim's face. I'm pretty good at detecting whatever sediment of sadness or anxiety or excitement lies just below his topsoil expression. So as I was walking toward him in the cafeteria, I was trying to see if there was anything about him that would give it away.

But as soon as I sat down he goes, "Your mom is still in a coma, but she's stabilized."

"Okay," I said, exhaling.

He looked tired. His shirt was wrinkled. He kept crossing and recrossing his hands. He didn't have his paper clip, and in my mind that's what accounted for his disheveled appearance, like his paper clip was some kind of tuning fork or antenna he needed to connect with the atmosphere.

"Well," he said, "I just wanted to give you an update." He sighed and sat back. "How are you holding up?"

I shrugged. "I dunno."

I felt hungry and jittery. I haven't eaten anything in days.

"You know" — he sat forward, reenergized — "there's no book on how you're supposed to act when your mom is in a coma."

"Yeah," I said, but not in a sarcastic way.

I looked around and considered, not for the first time, how much I hate the faint ketchup and cleaner scent of the cafeteria.

"So, what now?" I said.

He sat forward. "What do you mean?"

"I mean, *what now?* What do we do?"

"About your mom?"

I didn't say anything.

"I guess the thing to do when someone is in a coma is..." Jim studied his hands. He rubbed his face. "...just wait."

I was feeling more jittery. It doesn't seem possible that there can be such inertia after something like this happens. My mom is about to die and there we were, plunk down in the cafeteria with our straw words. And everything continues at its lame, creaking pace. I watched someone I'd never seen walk down the hallway, look at a piece of paper, and mouth something to themselves.

"I mean, what's going to happen to Refrigerator...I mean Steve? He's out at Lorton now right? Isn't that minimum security? When is he going to go to a bigger jail?"

When is he going to get beaten to death with a bunch of broken-off broom handles in a dirty bathroom? When is a serial rapist going to use a contraband razor to cut into his cheek like a piece of pie? When is each one of his arms and legs going to get shackled to a different planet, slowly orbiting away from one another?

I'd been gripping the sides of my chair so hard that my skin made a suction sound when I lifted my hands off.

Jim spread his fingers out on the table. He laughed a sad little laugh and shook his head. "You would think he would...," he said. And then he started stopping and starting. "The way these things work...the thing is, the system of justice can be very slow...but that *doesn't* mean that Steve Kensky isn't going to have to pay for what he's done." Jim jabbed the table. "Unfortunately, until he stands trial—"

"He's not in prison."

"Well..., someone posted the bail."

I pictured Refrigerator Man watching television in a musty living room, sitting in an inflatable pool raft.

"What the fuck? What was the bail? A pair of sweatpants?"

"I'm not sure exactly what it was. I think they set it pretty high. But apparently Steve has a brother out in Crozet."

I felt like a knife being sharpened. Then I felt my eyes pooling and I looked away from Jim. Then I felt like a knife being sharpened again.

"It's not ideal, obviously," Jim said. "But by posting bail he's agreed to show up in court. Until then, however...," he trailed off.

The same system of justice that slam-dunked me into these nauseatingly bright hallways is letting Refrigerator Man continue to roam the earth like a short-circuited bulldozer.

We sat in the cafeteria for a little while longer as Jim continued to do his thing. He moved his hands around, looked concerned, said he was going to be there for me no matter what happened. He did all the things he *would* do. And then, eventually, he left.

I pictured Refrigerator Man standing in a convenience store, holding a six-pack, trying to decide which snack to get with his beer, looking over all the choices. I see him pick something up, study it with his filmy eyes, and then walk it to the cash register. He sets the six-pack down on the counter only to decide he wants something different. Conveying this information with a grunt, he leaves everyone in line there to wait as he wades back to the snack aisle to make a decision.

I see him ambling down a sidewalk, hiccupping, looking from one house to the next. He finally ends up at me and my mom's, at the end of the street, with the cracked concrete walkway. He shoves the flimsy door open and walks inside as if he belonged there. He looks around, bewildered, makes his way to the kitchen and sits down in a chair. He yawns and cracks open a beer. A wave of irritation ripples through him. He slams his fist down on the table. Burps. Closes his eyes and finally drifts off to a dark, quilted place where you get away with everything.

I realize now that this is what it feels like to know that you could actually kill someone; in the light of day, in real time. I could drag that rock from point A to point B. I could do it and know I was doing it and see myself doing it from the outside and still finish, tying the package off and sending it to whatever fucked-up rubric of judgment actually exists if one does. I hate him.

Murderer Convention

I bet if you went to a convention of murderers, everyone would seem pretty normal at first. It would be a bunch of adults milling around, everyone at a different degree of grown-up frumpiness, standing in loose groups and drinking punch out of paper cups. There would be some teenagers and maybe even a few kids. People would talk to one another and use hand gestures. You would look across the room at someone and study them and maintain eye contact. Maybe it would be a bored-looking woman pulling a crumb off her sweater. Maybe it would be some red-faced old guy trying to remember a punch line, and you would wonder: Soldier or assassin? Serial killer or sniper? Who here has taken life under some official banner? Whose moments were more disorganized and improvised? Who killed in a frantic rage and who after years of quiet calculation, calcified jealousy, or seasonal, harvested hatred?

Maybe after standing around for a while you would see or talk to someone who reminded you of yourself—the way they spoke, their turns of phrase. You might get into a conversation that wasn't even about murdering but about something completely different. Like a vacation you once took, or about how you both knew the guy from a local car dealership commercial. Eventually you would think, This person isn't so bad. They probably killed because they had to. Or because whatever system of justice that was supposed to be in place hadn't acted swiftly enough or hadn't acted at all and therefore they had to take matters into their own hands. After all, couldn't some of the murders have been justified? It's not like everyone here at this convention is a *bad person*.

Then you would realize that there's one thing everyone here has in common. And that's that during that blind moment, or maybe it was a terribly lucid one, when each person picked up the object they would use to strum out a song of last breaths, there was a part of all of us that knew we were doing the right thing.

Anything Can Be a Weapon

That would be the main theme of the convention, the keynote subject. We would all sit around in circles and discuss what we had used. Some of them would be obvious — guns, knives, cars, crowbars. And some would be less obvious. How do people kill in the twenty-first century? You can still use a pillow, says an old woman. With words, someone else would say. With a years-long campaign of subtle insults and insinuations until she couldn't take it anymore. With an M-16 given to you after a few months of training and a flimsy promise of allegiance. A cliff, when no one is watching. Or a window, says a little kid. Even a top-floor window can be a weapon. By *not* doing something, says a man cleaning his glasses with his shirttail.

We would discuss how it was that we all came to be here. If it was true, perhaps, that we ourselves were weapons, being sharpened to a lethal point that whole time on the whetstone of our shitty lives. And could we help it? — that when the moment came, whether we liked it or not, we were locked and loaded.

No. We couldn't help it, we would all agree.

The lights would flicker off for a moment and then come back on. Everyone would laugh nervously and look around and shift in their seats.

What about you? we would say to one another. How did it all unfold?

I was sitting on the slumping couch in my apartment, watching a talk show, waiting for her to come home. I was standing there, and the wind was blowing, and there was no one around, and I saw an opportunity. I was waiting behind a car, and they all started filing out of the gym. You won't believe it, but it actually happened in a dark alley. She didn't know about the gun, even though I'd had it for more than six months. The knife felt like it was an extension of my own hands. I pushed him. I pushed her down. It was harder than I thought it was going to be. It was easy. It was exhilarating. Terrible. Like a dream. My hair felt hot. I blacked out for a second. There was a song stuck in my head, you know that one? The golden oldie? I pictured my parents. I didn't feel bad at all. I felt bad the whole time.

I was angry, I said.

Yup, they all nodded.

Do you know the feeling? Of being so angry? So angry you could tear your own eyes out? So angry you could rip carpets of land right off the earth?

Yes, yes, we know.

I hated my mother's boyfriend.

Classic, they would say. *Vintage.*

I was in a juvenile detention center.

Uh-huh.

And I knew someone who was going to set a fire.

Nice. Anguished suburban murder. Very midnineties.

He wanted everyone we knew to die, to burn to death. He thought they all deserved it. He wanted to see them run around.

We see.

I was so angry that I didn't care. I don't care. Why should I? Why should I care when everything stays the same no matter what? And I'm tired. Tired of thinking that things matter. Why should I care if someone could get hurt or even die?

You shouldn't.

Everyone thinks there's a Before and After, and maybe if you look at it close, it seems like what you do makes a difference. But when you step back you will see that Before and After don't exist, that they share the same peaks and valleys in an unfolding predetermined land; that everything was set before we even started and the only thing that Before and After do is make out in some philosophical pornography of How to Be a Person so that we have something to watch here on earth when really it doesn't matter. Nothing matters.

Amen.

Me and my friend, we once took something that wasn't ours. We watched as the person from whom we had taken this thing figured out that it wasn't there anymore. He stood staring silently into a fireplace among lots of other things that weren't his. What he needed was five feet away from him, buried in a bowl of fake apples and pears. I wonder about him. I wonder if he's alive or dead. I wonder what he was thinking as he was staring into the fireplace. I wonder if he thought his life was just *like that.*

Yes, yes. Now tell us about this fire.

I knew a guy who was going to try and burn everyone.

Go on.

He had this stupid plan. It didn't really make any sense. I knew it wasn't going to work. But . . .

But what?

I could tell he really wanted to hurt someone, anyone. You could see it when you looked at him. You could see him seeing himself hurting someone badly.

And...that's about it. Actually, I don't even know why I'm here. Because I didn't actually kill anyone.

Yes, you did, says the man cleaning his glasses with his shirt-tail. He looks up at me. His face is long and looks familiar. *Of course you did. Standing there and not doing anything is just as sharp a weapon as a knife. You're just like us.*

You're just like us, they all say, looking at me.

Now lets' go see about that buffet.

An Overturned Chair, a Wide Bowl, a Swatch of Fabric

There are only three people. They are standing in a triangle in a room, and they are very still. One of them is covered in linen, a linen animal. She is frozen, caught out of her environment. Her left hand is up in the air, as if to wave or push. Her right hand is making a fist and in the fist is a pencil with a little flag attached to it.

One of them is holding a chair, but the way he's holding it, it doesn't look like a chair. It looks like four steel spokes of an antenna, as if he's trying to communicate or wrangle a signal from the sky. His face is momentarily scrambled with confusion and then it slowly straightens out into a smile.

The third person is me. I'm by the door. I'm clutching a piece of paper. I feel sick to my stomach. There are thousands of ready-made treaties and fleeting threats bouncing around between us, in our triangle. We dart our eyes back and forth at each other. I've been in this rec room a million times. But now I feel like I'm on new land, and that everything we do, all strokes, will be historical and precedent-setting.

Four minutes ago I was walking down a hallway on my way with everyone else to the computer room. We were passing the cafeteria when David, from behind, goes, "Aaron." I've never heard him speak that loud before. His voice sounds warped and out of tune. I turn around, we make eye contact. I shake my head at him.

Two hours before that I'd been in the cafeteria. David was a few tables over, staring at me as he stabbed his food with his fork. Whenever I looked at him he gave me a conspiratorial little nod.

Five weeks before that, I held Andrea's hand.

Five months before that, I hit an old man in the head with a gun at three in the morning.

Six years before that, my mom and I moved to Virginia for no apparent reason.

Aaron looks back and stops.

"What?"

About two years before that, I found myself in a new house in Texas, standing in a hallway and looking at a drawing of a hawk flying down through a canyon. It was quiet and too clean and I wasn't supposed to be there and I remember thinking that all of these materials had accumulated to make this random house in this development in the middle of nowhere, and how was everything else going to turn out?

"Go back and get my outline worksheet?" says David. "Left it there."

"He can use mine," I say, the words rolling out of me. "He can...we're working together."

Aaron looks confused and annoyed.

David and I start talking at the same time. We stop. David says, "I forgot something."

Aaron looks distracted. His face unlocks with resignation and then hardens again.

"That's too bad," he says, turning around. "You should have remembered."

I look back at David. He's stopped in his tracks as everyone continues walking. When I look back again, he's gone.

I'm thinking, There's no way what David thinks is going to happen is actually going to happen. I'm thinking, There are a million ways the next ten minutes could unfold, what is the possibility that someone could actually get hurt? My face feels warm. Everything is too loud. My heart is beating. I see myself from the outside and then I look down at my legs and it turns out I am doing what I thought I was doing. I've stopped. In the two-second interim when the group has turned the corner and I'm out of Aaron's vision, I've turned and started walking the other way. My legs—I feel like I'm underwater. Jamie looks at me and mouths, *"What are you doing?"* I start running.

Or it's really like a jog. I'm looking from side to side in the bright hallways. Expecting to smell smoke. Expecting to see people running around with horrible expressions on their faces. But everything is quiet and normal. I don't have any sense of proportion.

The first thing I see when I approach the rec room is Lane. She's standing there, next to the sofa, transfixed by something in front of her. She's got the pencil in one of her hands. I move closer and see David holding the chair, its legs out, up in the air, like he means to charge. I smell carpet cleaner. Neither of them seems to notice I'm there.

I can feel us making our way down the sides of a huge bowl, about to meet in the middle. I wonder how long it is that we've all been sliding.

Lane says, "David."

David says, "Shut up."

He's rocking back and forth on his feet a little. And Lane has started to rapidly blink her eyes. I listen for sounds of people coming but there's nothing behind me or in the hallway.

David, without turning his head says, "Jacob."

Lane looks at me like she's never seen me before. Or that's not exactly it. She looks at me as if she's not sure what to recognize; she's not sure if she's in twice the amount of danger, if I'm part of this. Because, her expression tells me, I could be a part of this. I could be allied with David. And us meeting here could be part of the whole plan.

David looks at me and says, "C'mon."

I wonder if it's obvious to Lane, deep down inside, what I'm going to do, or not going to do. Or if it will be obvious only after it's done.

David is still looking at me and his features are now floating apart, like parcels in a sinking ship. He says, "Come *on*," in a completely different way.

You ever do anything? You ever jump off a dock into a lake? When you break it down, the motion, the energy it takes, isn't much more or less than anything else. But it's hard to know when to jump when you're staring down at your toes. The seconds pass like train cars and you feel a mounting pressure to pick one.

Lane says, "Put the chair down."

David has recomposed himself and now his face is stretching into that caustic smile.

"Why?"

"Because —"

"I'm so happy," he interrupts.

You do these instinctive calculations, you don't even know that you're doing them: if you've got the right amount of liftoff to propel you the right amount of distance. And even though you're just standing, you wonder if everything in your life has been pushing you here.

"Happy that I found you all," he says. He lunges forward with the chair.

Then, when it finally happens, it's the funniest thing. Each millisecond afterward, in each beat of memory that takes you back even as you're flying through the air, you still can't believe you really did it.

I say a word, it clunks up into my mouth, I form its awkward corners and I yell it, I leap forward and yell, "Stop!" as he charges at Lane. She staggers back into a bookshelf. The chair hits me, hard, on the side of the forehead. And then I'm on the floor. My face is being pushed into the carpet and I'm surrounded by a forest of legs. I focus on the bottom of someone's pants. People are yelling. I study the intersecting fibers. I close my eyes.

Lights out.

Two Months, Three Weeks, Six Days Later

Tips for the Savvy Senior: Ideas and Suggestions for the 50+ Crowd

Topics include personal safety, identity fraud, assisted living options, emergency preparation, and more. Keynote speaker Janet Simon-Cox will read from her book *Over 50?! Fine by Me.* 8 p.m., Kingston Library, $8.00 for nonmembers, $4.00 for members.

This is just one of the entries I had to make today in my cubicle at the *Braddock Gazette Packet*, as part of my boring new job as assistant calendar editor. This place isn't without perks, though. For instance: I don't have to ask anyone if I can go to the bathroom. Also, there is an apparently unlimited supply of toffees on the receptionist's desk. Those, along with the free coffee in the break room, allow me enough of a hollow, sweaty, amphetamine buzz to complete most of what I have to do in random fits and starts throughout the day.

Perplexing Perennials and Dastardly Daffodils:

Learn how to avoid common garden gaffes and make your yard come alive! Session two of a five-class series. All are welcome. 7 p.m., Braddock County Community Center.

Because of my frequent trips to her desk for toffees, Jenny, the receptionist, is one of the few people I talk to here.

"Back for more," she'll say, staring at her computer screen.

"Yup, gotta fix up." I'll fish around in the bowl for a vanilla-flavored one because that is my favorite.

"I'd be careful, toffees are a gateway candy."

"Whatever," I'll say. "I'm just having fun, but I know when to stop." I'll unwrap it and eat it right there, stuffing the wrapper in my pocket. "Why? You got anything stronger?"

"Well," she'll say, looking at herself in a compact mirror and pulling at her eyelashes, "I'm talking to my supplier out at the Shop 'n Save for something that's a little harder to get a hold of. Three words: chocolate. mint. wafers."

"Oh, shit," I'll say. "I want in on that."

"We'll see." She snaps her compact closed.

Jenny is twenty-eight years old and was in the middle of getting her PhD in religious studies at George Mason University but then decided to quit and now she works here. She has straight, pretty hair. Her desk is shaped like a car with the opened convertible roof serving as a sort of hutch for her computer.

"Why is your desk shaped like a car?" I once asked her.

"I don't know," she said. "But I'm about to drive it off an overpass."

Jim was able to get me this job as part of the Transitional Living Program they stuck me in after I left the center. He's good friends with someone who works here, and so even though it's labeled as an internship because I don't have any qualifications, for now they're giving me minimum wage. Everyone has been pretty nice so far. There's no one watching me all the time. I'll have the instinct to look up and locate the little camera in the ceiling but there isn't one. Every once in a while, the actual calendar editor, a very soft-spoken guy named Dale Greene, will shamble over and ask if I need anything. He's the one who showed me what I need to do, how to summarize the releases we get from different community centers and nonprofits and local theaters and format them into calendar entries.

He also said that once I've worked here for a little while, I could maybe write an actual article, a community-interest piece or something like that. At first I was like, "Yeah right, why would anyone try to do that?" But then I thought of this park we used to go to in high school, out on Route 1, close to where they're building the new Herndon Town Center. It's acres and acres of dusty green spilling out into the distance. Then here and there, emerging from the ground, are sculptures. They all stand very still in the rippling grass, like monuments to different religions. I thought maybe I could write about that.

Jim came over yesterday. Because Erin's still in the hospital, he's been helping me with all the mail and bills and things that come to the house. (He gave me a folder to put them in and I was like, "Boring!") He brought Amy and they made me hold their freakish alien baby, otherwise known as June. She was heavy and warm.

Jim said that he'd gone to visit Erin, that she can move her legs and squeeze a foam ball with her hand now. He said that she was doing better every day, but that they still weren't sure if there was going to be permanent damage, that only time would tell. He said it was getting more and more difficult to make excuses for why I hadn't been back to visit. I did go once. It was back when I first got out of the center. Jim took me. She was still asleep and her face looked like a blanket that had billowed out and resettled the wrong way. We only stayed for a few minutes.

The events following that day in the rec room, the day David tried to start a fire, get scrambled in my brain, and so sometimes, every once in a while, I try to straighten them out.

After David charged at Lane, and I ran between them and got hit in the head with a chair, Officer O'Connell and Aaron came and found us there and slammed us down onto the ground, and I was taken to my room. I was there for a really long time. Every now and then, someone would come and check on me. But I didn't really know what was going on, or what was going to happen, until Jim came to talk to me.

"You're not in any trouble," he said.

"Okay," I said.

I was lying on my bed with my hands on my stomach, looking up.

"Lane is fine. She hit the back of her head, but she's fine."

"Okay."

I stared at the specks on the ceiling. My head hurt.

"They took David away. They're going to want to talk to you. But all you have to do is tell them what happened."

"Okay," I said. "How far do I go back?"

I spoke to Andrea on the phone. It was like trying to open a can without a can opener. I couldn't hear her that well and we kept interrupting each other. She said she was standing in line at a gelato place. She was like, "Should I get passion fruit? Or bourbon vanilla?" I was like, "What!" She goes, "Bourbon vanilla! Passion fruit!"

She told me that she was going back to school. We're supposed to hang out next week. I don't know who is supposed to call who, though.

I've got the first few sentences of this article I want to write on that park. I wrote them and then I couldn't think of where to go from there. I sit at my computer and stare at the words. Someone will walk by and I'll click over to the calendar program so that I look busy, but then I'll click back.

Everyone else has things on their desk. Little plants, photographs, a lava lamp. One person has the Mexican flag. Another thing is that there's a trash can next to my chair that gets changed every day even if there's nothing in it. Sometimes there's a Styrofoam cup, or some candy wrappers, but it never fills up. And then every morning when I come in, it's got a new lining with the sides tied tightly around the rim. I never see the person who changes them. They must go around after everyone leaves. I want to tell them that they can relax a little.

It's like a traffic jam of words on my computer that I don't know how to get out of. I don't know how to break it up and make it malleable. I don't know what thought is supposed to come naturally after another. I stare at the screen. I scratch at a stain on my desk. I crack my knuckles. I lean back and yawn. I listen to the white noise of conversations around the room. I look back at my computer. I think of the person coming around and changing all the trash can liners every day. The thing is, I still don't know what it is that people *do*.

Acknowledgments

I'd like to thank these people for their encouragement and guidance: Adam Brock, Gina Welch, Jim Rutman, Oliver Haslegrave, Andrea Walker, Reagan Arthur, Eve Attermann, Marlena Bittner, my family, Poldi, Danie, Melanie, Ben, and Dan, and my teachers and peers at the University of Virginia.

About the Author

EMMA RATHBONE is a graduate of New York University and the MFA Fiction Program at the University of Virginia. She currently lives in Charlottesville and is beginning work on a second novel.

Reading Group Guide

The Patterns of Paper Monsters

A novel by

EMMA RATHBONE

A conversation with Emma Rathbone

How did Jacob emerge to you as a character?

Jacob started as a voice more than anything else. I originally imagined the novel as a series of inappropriate and very angry columns he would write for the newsletter at the juvenile detention center. It was really fun to write with so much sarcasm about the little details of the place—the food, the posters on the wall, and so on. Then I realized the column format was unrealistic and unsustainable, so I kept the nature of the voice and changed it to journal entries. That's when Jacob really opened up as a character for me, because I could talk about his past and his innermost thoughts and just basically get really personal. And that exploration, the sort of mapping of his mental topography, was one of the most rewarding aspects of writing the book.

How did you know what the day-to-day environment in a northern Virginia juvenile detention center would be like?

Well, the massive high school I went to in northern Virginia was rumored to have once been a prison (the barbed wire above the fence surrounding the football field didn't dissuade anyone from this idea). Whether or not it really was, it was of the same institutional public cartilage as all the court buildings in the area. So from that experience I already had a template in my mind of what the JDC would look like.

But I did do some research, too. I was lucky because at the time my mom was working in the court system and was able to set me up with someone who gave me a tour of an actual youth corrections facility. I got to ask a lot of questions about the routine and procedures. Not only that, but walking through the hallways and looking into the rooms solidified my ideas of how the center in my book would look and feel. And my mom passed an early version of the manuscript on to someone she knew in the system, who gave me some pointers.

What is your writing process like? Do you write every day or whenever inspiration strikes?

A lot of writers say their most productive time is the morning, and that seems to be true for me, too. My writing process involves a lot of staring at the screen and a lot of little breaks. Sometimes I write in a notebook and then type up what I've written because adding an arbitrary step makes me feel like I'm being really productive.

I do try to write every day. I don't believe in the mentality of writing only when you're inspired—partly because if I did that, I wouldn't get anything done, and partly because I've found that when I'm dizzy with some idea, the writing isn't really any better than when I'm sitting there in the sober light of morning, slowly knocking something out.

How much do you revise?

Revision is a huge part of my writing. Revision and time. I've learned that one of the most important things I can do is also one of the hardest—and that's to put something away for a while. It's almost like I need to forget a passage or a chapter and then look at it again with new eyes. And that's when I find I can see what I really have, where the possibilities are, what needs to be cut, enhanced, and so forth. Revision isn't actually so bad. That feeling where you look at something again and finally, finally, realize where it needs to go is unbeatable.

You were born in South Africa and have lived in places as varied as Texas, New York City, and Virginia. Has that movement affected your work?

I think perhaps moving did affect my writing in that the contrast between the places I have lived has allowed me to see each of them more clearly, and therefore I could write about northern Virginia, for instance, with a sharper perspective.

What is the importance of humor to you as a writer? Did you know in the early stages of writing The Patterns of Paper Monsters *that you wanted it to have strong comic elements?*

I didn't set out to write a funny book. But I like to read things that are funny. And it's especially satisfying when that funny thing has some startling zing of truth to it. So I did try to do that. The humor is largely what kept me anchored in the book. Because writing is so hard for so many reasons, the moments when you're actually having fun (thinking of word choices or how you're going to nail a description) really help.

What do you most hope readers will take away from the experience of reading your novel?

It would mean a lot to me to have created something that people enjoyed. Also, it would be great if when reading the book people felt like I did when writing it — that Jacob had become a friend.

Questions and topics for discussion

1. How would you describe Jacob's attitude to his incarceration in the juvenile detention center at the start of the novel?

2. Describe Jacob's first series of encounters with Andrea. Why are they drawn to each other? Discuss the ways in which their relationship develops.

3. What is the importance of Jacob's recollections of Rocky, the friend with whom he used to break into houses in Texas?

4. How does the author use humor to shape your impression of such characters as Lane and Janet Stipling?

5. Describe your first impressions of David. Is he ever a sympathetic character in spite of his malevolence?

6. How do you think Jacob's relationship with his mother has shaped his view of the world? How do you think their individual outlooks change in the course of the novel?

7. Why do you think Jim Dade joins the Second Cousins program? What do you think he and Jacob learn from each other?

8. How does the novel's northern Virginia setting influence its characters?

9. What is the importance of Jacob's dialogue with Pastor Todd about individual choice?

10. Discuss the novel's ending. Where do you see Jacob in five years? In ten years?

Emma Rathbone's suggestions
for further reading

These are some of the books I read as a teenager. They're the kinds of books Jacob might read, and they may have contributed to the development of his voice.

1984 by George Orwell
This is one of the first "grown-up" books that I can remember reading and being riveted by in that not-noticing-the-light-in-the-room-is-getting-dimmer-and-dimmer-until-someone-comes-in-and-switches-on-a-lamp-and-you-realize-you've-been-reading-in-the-dark-for-two-hours kind of way.

The Martian Chronicles by Ray Bradbury
I was swept away by Bradbury's vision of Mars in this book. But the thing that stayed with me the most is the book's undercurrent of sadness as men trying to colonize the planet bash in everything sacred about it.

High Weirdness by Mail by Rev. Ivan Stang
This book, written in the eighties, is a pre-Internet catalog of the outlandish things you can (or could) send away for in the mail, from New Age religious tracts to government-conspiracy zines. It's funny and sarcastic, and it expanded my knowledge of the bizarre backwaters of American culture.

The Rachel Papers by Martin Amis
It is a lot of fun to be in the pyrotechnic mind of Charles Highway on the occasion of his twentieth birthday.

The Trial by Franz Kafka
I'm sure I wasn't the only teenager who could relate to Joseph K. and his persecution by an unchecked bureaucratic body, or, in my case, high school.

Generation X by Douglas Coupland
Filled with hyperarticulate characters, this was one of the first books I encountered that described a sort of whiplash from growing up with so much information. I didn't know you were "allowed" to write so specifically about the layers of your own cultural moment.

Neuromancer by William Gibson
I was a big fan of dystopian future landscapes as a teenager, and I was astounded by the intricacy and imagination of this cyberspace epic involving a burned-out computer hacker named Case and his bad-ass girlfriend, Molly Millions.

CivilWarLand in Bad Decline by George Saunders
These stories evoke such a specific and corroded landscape and were different from anything I'd encountered. Also, George Saunders straddles the funny/sad divide better than anyone I've read.

The Sun Also Rises by Ernest Hemingway
This book made me want to go to Europe. And also live in a completely different time period. I thought Brett Ashley was really sophisticated, and I was attracted to Hemingway's lean conversational prose.